He kept coming, st

Before she could object, he hauled her into his arms and swung her in a wide circle.

"Put me down before you hurt yourself. More. Again."

"I did it!"

"Ethan, please!"

He released her. Except the moment her feet touched the ground, he lowered his mouth to hers, stopping a fraction of an inch shy of kissing her.

"I've wanted to do this for the past three days."

Three days? Was that all?

She'd been waiting the past eight years, eleven months and twenty-one days to kiss him.

Dear Reader,

If asked, I would admit that reunion stories are one of my favorite kinds to read—which made *Her Cowboy's Christmas Wish* one of my favorite kind to write. From the moment I began this book I knew Ethan Powell would be an interesting guy. How could a former rodeo bronc rider trying for a comeback after a long stint in the marines not be interesting? Only when he first appeared on the pages of *Last Chance Cowboy* did I realize Ethan returned from the Middle East minus the lower half of his left leg.

I wondered how his family and friends might look at him and if they'd treat him differently. I was really curious how his old high school sweetheart would react when she first saw him. While imagining that scene, Caitlin Carmichael came to life for me. She is strong, yet scared to death and not at all the person she was when she and Ethan dated those many years ago. Then again, neither is he.

Helping these two people rekindle their love, resolve their differences and find their meant-to-be happily-ever-after has been pure pleasure for me. I hope reading their story is for you, too.

Warmest wishes,

Cathy McDavid

P.S. I always enjoy hearing from readers. You can contact me at www.cathymcdavid.com.

Her Cowboy's
Christmas Wish

CATHY McDAVID

TORONTO NEW YORK LONDON
AMSTERDAM PARIS SYDNEY HAMBURG
STOCKHOLM ATHENS TOKYO MILAN MADRID
PRAGUE WARSAW BUDAPEST AUCKLAND

Recycling programs
for this product may
not exist in your area.

ISBN-13: 978-0-373-75388-8

HER COWBOY'S CHRISTMAS WISH

Copyright © 2011 by Cathy McDavid

This edition published by arrangement with Harlequin Books S.A.

For questions and comments about the quality of this book
please contact us at Customer_eCare@Harlequin.ca

® and TM are trademarks of the publisher. Trademarks indicated with
® are registered in the United States Patent and Trademark Office, the
Canadian Trade Marks Office and in other countries.

www.Harlequin.com

Printed in U.S.A.

ABOUT THE AUTHOR

Cathy makes her home in Scottsdale, Arizona, near the breathtaking McDowell Mountains where hawks fly overhead, javelina traipse across her front yard and mountain lions occasionally come calling. She embraced the country life at an early age, acquiring her first horse in eighth grade. Dozens of horses followed through the years, along with mules, an obscenely fat donkey, chickens, ducks, goats and a pot-bellied pig who had her own swimming pool. Nowadays, two spoiled dogs and two spoiled-er cats round out the McDavid pets. Cathy loves contemporary and historical ranch stories and often incorporates her own experiences into her books.

When not writing, Cathy and her family and friends spend as much time as they can at her cabin in the small town of Young. Of course, she takes her laptop with her on the chance inspiration strikes.

Books by Cathy McDavid

HARLEQUIN AMERICAN ROMANCE

*Mustang Valley

Don't miss any of our special offers. Write to us at the following address for information on our newest releases.

Harlequin Reader Service
U.S.: 3010 Walden Ave., P.O. Box 1325, Buffalo, NY 14269
Canadian: P.O. Box 609, Fort Erie, Ont. L2A 5X3

To my own darling Caitlin.
You were truly the most beautiful baby ever born.
I'm not exactly sure when you grew up into this
incredible, lovely and supersmart young woman,
but it happened. And I couldn't be any prouder.
Love you forever, Mom.

Chapter One

The big buckskin reared—at least he tried to rear. His thick, rangy body was too confined by the narrow chute, so he achieved little height. Frustrated, he pawed the ground, then backed up and banged into the panel with such force the reverberation carried down the metal railing like an electrical current.

"He's an ornery one," the cowboy sitting astride the fence said. "And smarter than he looks."

Ethan Powell considered the man's assessment of the horse he was about to ride, and decided he agreed. The buckskin was ornery and smart, and would enjoy nothing better than stomping Ethan into the ground.

Exactly the kind of saddle bronc he preferred. The kind he'd hoped to draw when he'd competed professionally. Nowadays his rodeo riding was restricted to this small, local arena and for "personal enjoyment" only. No sanctioned rodeo, or unsanctioned rodeo for that matter, would allow him to enter.

He understood. He just didn't like it, and was determined to change the Duvall Rodeo Arena's policies, if not the entire Professional Rodeo Cowboys Association. Before he could do that, however, he had to prove he still had what it took to go up against men who were, for the most part, younger than him and, without exception, physically whole.

"You gonna stand there all night, Powell?" the cowboy asked.

In the chute beside Ethan, the buckskin lifted his head and stared straight ahead, every muscle in his body bunched tight with anticipation.

Just like Ethan.

"Yeah, I'm ready."

Shielding his eyes from the bright floodlights that lit the arena, he climbed the fence and straddled it alongside the wrangler. Then he took another few seconds to study the bronc up close.

"Good luck," the cowboy said.

Ethan would need more than luck if he expected to ride this bad boy for eight seconds.

He'd been on plenty of unbroken and green broke horses in the last year. There was, however, a world of difference between those animals and one bred and trained to give a man the ride of his life.

Drawing a deep breath, he braced a hand on either side of the chute and lowered himself onto the buckskin's back inch by inch. Twice he paused, waiting for the big horse to settle. Once in the saddle, he took hold of the reins and slipped his feet into the stirrups, careful to keep his toes pointed forward.

The buckskin, eager to give his rider a preview of what was to come, twisted sideways. Ethan's left ankle was momentarily pinned between the horse's broad body and the chute. It might have hurt if he had any feeling in his lower leg.

He didn't and probably never would, unless medical science developed a prosthetic device with artificial nerve endings that could transmit sensation to the wearer.

When his ankle was freed and the buckskin was once

again in position, Ethan slid the reins back and forth through his gloved hands until the grip felt right.

The moment the horse committed, he nodded to the wrangler manning the gate and said, "Go," hoping like heck he wasn't making a huge mistake.

With a loud metallic whoosh the gate slid open. Ethan tried to straighten his legs and set his spurs. He didn't quite make it. The prosthesis he wore failed to respond as quickly as his real leg did.

The buckskin lunged out of the chute and into the arena. Only his front feet touched the ground. His hind ones were raised high above his head as he tried to kick the moon out of the sky.

Ethan didn't have time to mark his horse, much less find his rhythm. With his weight unevenly distributed, the buckskin easily unseated him and sent him sailing through the air. Ethan barely glimpsed the ground as it came rushing up to meet him.

His shoulder absorbed the brunt of the impact, which he supposed was better than his face or prosthetic leg. That was until he moved. Pain, razor sharp and searing hot, ripped through him. He decided it was better to just lie there for a second or two longer.

Shouting, which seemed to come from far away, told him the buckskin had been safely rounded up and was probably gloating.

"Need help?"

Ethan glanced up, then away. What he'd dreaded the most had just happened.

"Nope, I'm fine," he told the pickup man looming above him. At least the guy hadn't gotten off his horse before offering his assistance. That would have been even more humiliating.

Ethan pushed up on one elbow, the one not throbbing,

then climbed to his knees. Getting his good leg under him was a little tricky, especially given the way the world was spinning. He could feel the eyes of the crowd on him, with everyone likely wondering if he was going to rise under his own power and take on another bronc.

The answer was *damn straight.*

In a minute, after he could move his shoulder and arm without having flashes of color pulsate before his eyes.

"The first time's the hardest," the pickup man commented.

"So they say."

Except this wasn't Ethan's first time bronc riding. It was his first time since losing his leg fifteen months ago, while serving in the Middle East. He'd loved the marines almost as much as he loved rodeoing. Now both were lost to him.

Maybe not rodeoing, he corrected himself.

Standing upright, he brushed off his jeans and readjusted his hat, which had miraculously stayed on during the fall. Then he walked to the gate, doing his best not to limp. It wasn't easy. Another cowboy held the gate open for him and clapped him on the back as he passed. The resulting pain almost drove Ethan to his knees, but he didn't so much as blink.

Outside the arena, he paused to catch his breath. This wasn't going exactly as planned.

"Hey, Ethan!"

He lifted his head to see his childhood friend Clay Duvall approaching, his gait brisk as usual. Ethan and Clay had been close up until their early twenties, when Ethan's mother had died from complications following a heart transplant, and Clay's father had sold Ethan's family's land out from under them. Ethan had joined the marines and for almost eight years neither saw nor spoke to his former friend. His anger at the Duvalls had been too great.

It was Clay, however, who gave him the opportunity to

realize his ambition of bronc riding again, along with a job breaking and training his rodeo stock. After a chance meeting with Clay three months ago, Ethan had realized he couldn't hold a twenty-one-year-old kid responsible for his father's actions, and the two had reconciled.

It had taken Ethan's brother, Gavin, longer to get over his animosity toward Clay. But now the two were partners in a mustang stud and breeding business, with Clay owning the wild mustang stallion and Gavin the mares.

Sometimes, when the three men were together, it felt as if all those years they'd been at odds with each other had never happened.

Ethan pushed off the railing, doing his best not to wince as invisible knife blades sliced through his shoulder. "How you doing?"

"I was going to ask you the same question." Clay grinned good-naturedly. "That was quite a fall you took."

"I'll survive." Ethan rolled his shoulders. Big mistake. He sucked in air through his teeth and waited for the spasm to pass.

"What say we have the new nurse check you out?"

"Nurse?"

Clay hitched his chin in the direction of the empty announcer's stand. "She's here setting up the first-aid station for the jackpot."

"I thought you were bringing in an EMT and an ambulance."

"Too expensive. Found out I could hire a nurse for a lot less money and still meet the insurance company's requirement for providing on-site emergency care."

Ethan resisted. "I'm fine." He didn't want to be checked out. And he sure didn't want the other cowboys seeing him head for the first-aid station.

"Come on." Clay took a step in that direction. "We have a deal."

They did. Clay had agreed to let Ethan practice bronc riding as long as several conditions were met, one being that he have any injury examined by a medical professional. Ethan knew what a liability he was, that his chances of hurting himself were far greater than the next cowboy's. Clay was taking a sizable risk despite the waiver Ethan had signed.

If he didn't comply with his friend's conditions, there was no way on earth he'd be allowed to compete in the upcoming jackpot, much less practice for it.

Grumbling, he fell into step beside Clay, and the two of them headed toward the announcer's stand.

"You going to be ready in time?"

"Count on it." Ethan had until the Saturday after Thanksgiving, less than two weeks away, to last a full eight seconds on one of Clay's broncs. That was another of the conditions Ethan had to meet in order to enter the jackpot. "I'll be here every evening if I have to."

The door to the small room beneath the announcer's stand stood ajar. A minivan was backed up to it, the rear hatch open. As they neared, Ethan glimpsed plastic containers and cardboard boxes stacked inside the van and a handicap placard dangling from the rearview mirror.

Clay stopped suddenly and scratched the back of his neck, the movement tipping his cowboy hat forward over his furrowed brow.

"Something the matter?" Ethan asked.

"I was going to surprise you. Now I'm thinking that's not such a good idea."

"Surprise me with what?"

"My new nurse. You know her." He smiled ruefully. "That is, you used to know her. Pretty well, in fact."

Ethan had only a second to prepare before a young woman appeared in the doorway. She paused at the sight of him, recognition lighting her features.

Caitlin Carmichael.

She looked the same. Okay, maybe not the same, he decided on second thought. Nine years was a long time, after all. But she was as pretty as ever.

Her former long blond hair had darkened to a honey-brown and was cut in one of those no-nonsense short styles. Her clothing was equally functional—loose-fitting sweats beneath a down-filled vest. It was her green eyes, he noticed, that had changed the most. Once alive with mischief and merriment, they were now somber and guarded.

Something had happened to her during the years since they'd dated.

Was she thinking the same thing about him?

He waited for her glance to travel to his left leg. It didn't. Either she was very good at hiding her reactions or she hadn't heard about his injury.

"Hello, Ethan," she said, her voice slightly unsteady. "It's good to see you." She came forward, her hand extended. "Clay told me you were back in Mustang Valley and training horses for him."

"For a while now." He took her hand in his, remembering when their greetings and farewells had included a hug and a kiss. Often a long kiss.

An awkward silence followed, and he finally released her hand. "So, you're a nurse?"

She smiled. "I suppose that's hard to believe."

"A little." The mere sight of blood used to make her queasy. "I guess people change."

"They do." Her gaze went to his leg, answering Ethan's earlier question. She quickly looked away.

"I work mornings at the middle school and afternoons at

the new urgent-care clinic in Mustang Village," she continued. "Have since the school year started."

"And now for Clay, too."

Her cheeks colored.

Why? Ethan wondered. It was on the tip of his tongue to
ask how her husband or boyfriend felt about her busy schedule. Then it occurred to him maybe she and Clay were seeing
each other. That would explain the embarrassment.

Ethan couldn't blame his friend. And it wasn't as if he
had any kind of claim on Caitlin himself. Not after leaving
her high and dry when he'd enlisted, following his mother's
death.

"Speaking of which," Clay interjected, "Ethan's your first
patient."

Her eyebrows rose. "You are?"

"It's nothing," Ethan insisted, sending his friend—soon to
be *ex*-friend once again if he kept this up—a warning look.

He'd hardly gotten over the shock of seeing Caitlin. No
way was he ready to be examined by her.

Any choice he had in the matter was taken from him when
Clay all but shoved him through the door and into the dimly
lit room.

The next instant, his friend was gone, leaving Ethan
alone with the woman whose heart he'd broken, and who
still owned a very large piece of his.

CAITLIN PULLED A FLIMSY metal folding chair into the center
of the space and indicated Ethan should sit.

Gripping the back of the chair, he tested its strength. The
legs wobbled. "You sure?"

She shrugged apologetically. "I'm still setting up." When
he hesitated, she added, "There's always the cot."

He promptly sat, his long legs stretched out in front of
him, his big frame dwarfing the chair. Ethan had always

been tall, some had said too tall for a bronc or bull rider. What he'd done since they last saw each other was fill out. No longer lean and lanky, he'd grown into a wall of solid muscle. She supposed his two—or was it three?—overseas tours were responsible.

The extra weight looked good on him.

Who was she kidding? He just plain looked good.

Dark eyes, jet-black hair and a five o'clock shadow that should have looked scruffy but somehow managed to be sexy. And that smile of his. It had dazzled her at age seventeen, and never stopped during the four years they'd dated.

Wait. On second thought, he hadn't smiled yet.

He'd been pleasant and polite, but that devil-may-care charm was noticeably absent.

"I'm guessing you injured yourself?"

"My left shoulder," he said.

"Strained it?"

"Or something."

She stood in front of him and gently placed her hand on the afflicted area. He jerked at her touch.

"Does that hurt?"

"Some."

She suspected her proximity was responsible for his reaction more than anything else. There was a lot of history between them, after all, much of it unresolved.

"What happened?" She gently probed his shoulder.

"A horse decided he didn't much like me riding him."

It was on the tip of her tongue to ask how he managed that with a prosthetic leg, but she refrained. Clay had warned her that Ethan didn't appreciate reminders of his handicap, and refused to let it hold him back. Well, he'd always been competitive. First high school sports, then professional rodeo after graduation.

"Did you at least land on soft ground?"

"The arena."

"Thank goodness." She lifted his arm. "Tell me when it starts to hurt."

He said nothing, even when she raised it clear over his head. The clenching of his jaw told another story. She lowered his arm, then raised it again, this time to the side.

He squeezed his eyes shut, but remained stubbornly silent.

Bending his arm at the elbow, she pressed his hand into the small of his back. "What about now?"

"Okay." He released a long breath and shook off her grasp. "You win. It hurts."

So he wasn't invincible.

"You should see your doctor as soon as possible and get an X-ray," she told him, lightly massaging his shoulder. "You might have torn a ligament or your rotator cuff."

"I'll be better by morning."

He was back to being the tough guy.

"No, you're going to be worse. Trust me."

"I'll take some ibuprofen."

"Three a day, extra strength. Up to six if your stomach can tolerate it. Ice the shoulder for at least an hour tonight before you go to bed, and again in the morning. When you can't stand the pain anymore and decide I'm right, see your doctor."

He chuckled, and the smile she'd been missing earlier appeared, if only a shadow of the one she remembered.

"You have nothing to prove, Ethan." She laid her palm on his good shoulder. "See a doctor."

"You're wrong." He rose from the chair, either her touch or her words galvanizing him. "I do have something to prove."

One step on his part and they were standing toe to toe.

Unable to help herself, Caitlin looked up into his face. As his gaze raked over her, lingered on her mouth, the atmosphere surrounding them went from calm to highly charged.

So much for believing the attraction had died.

She retreated on unsteady legs. All these years apart, and he still had the ability to unsettle her.

"How's your family?" she asked. Breathing came easier with some distance between them. "Clay mentioned your brother's getting married."

"This spring. I suppose Clay also mentioned the two of them are partners in a stud and breeding business."

"No." By unspoken agreement, she and Ethan made their way to the door. "We really haven't talked much other than about setting up the first-aid station."

"Huh. I thought maybe you and he…"

"He and I what?"

"Had kept in touch." Ethan stepped aside, allowing her to precede him outside.

"We did up until he got married and moved away. I had no idea he was divorced and back in town."

"Then how did you wind up working for him?"

"He showed up at the school last Wednesday and asked me to run the first-aid station."

"Have you been at the school long?" They stopped beside her minivan.

"You really don't know?"

"Should I?"

"I thought maybe someone told you."

Mustang Village was a horse-friendly residential community, built in and named after Mustang Valley, the land Ethan's family had once owned, and where they had raised cattle for four generations. Their ranch, what was left of it, lay nestled in the foothills of the McDowell Mountains, and looked down on the village. Caitlin didn't think much happened that the Powells didn't know about.

She'd certainly heard about Ethan's injury, medical discharge and return home.

"I've worked at the school since August," she told him.

"That long?" he said, more to himself than her.

"Clay told me you're breaking horses for him."

"Trying to." Another half smile appeared. "Some of them aren't embracing the process."

"If anyone can change their minds, you can." Again she wondered how he managed such a physically demanding job. "Is your sister still living in San Francisco?"

"For five years now."

"But she visits, right?"

"Used to. Not much the last couple years."

"That's too bad."

"Sierra being gone so much is hard on Dad. He misses her. Misses Mom, too. Though he's doing a lot better lately since Cassie came to live with us. He's crazy about her."

Caitlin had met Ethan's twelve-year-old niece at the school. "I don't imagine recovering from the death of a loved one is ever easy."

"It's not."

The mention of his late mother put a damper on their conversation. It was right after Louise Powell died that Ethan had abruptly enlisted, leaving Caitlin to suffer the loss of not only a dear friend, but the love of her life.

A painful pressure built inside her chest.

Heartache.

It had been a long time since the memory of those unhappy days had caused such a profound physical reaction.

"How's your brother?" Ethan asked. "Gavin told me about the accident."

More pressure.

Discussing Justin was always hard for Caitlin. No matter how many obstacles he overcame and how many challenges he conquered, she could never forget that she was responsible for him being a paraplegic and having to spend the rest of his life in a wheelchair.

"He's graduating from Arizona State in December," she said, focusing on the positive. "With a master's in education."

"Good for him."

"We're all very proud. Now if he can just land a job."

"It's a tough economy."

"That, too."

Great strides had been made in the last few decades when it came to equal rights for handicapped employees, but Caitlin still worried about her brother's chances at finding decent employment.

Ethan distracted her by reaching into the back of her minivan and removing a carton of supplies.

"Hey, what are you doing?" She tried to take the box from him.

He swung it out of her reach. "Helping you unload."

"Ethan!" She sighed with exasperation. "You're hurt."

"My shoulder. Not my hands." He squeezed past her and carried his load inside.

She hurried after him.

"Where do you want this?"

Because she knew arguing with him was useless, she pointed to the folding table along the wall. "There. And don't even think about carrying anything else in."

He not only thought about it, he did it. She gave up and pitched in. Together, they quickly emptied the van.

"You're going to regret this tomorrow," she told him when they were done.

"You were never such a worrier before."

"It comes from being a nurse. So does being bossy." She leveled a finger at him. "Now get yourself home and take care of that shoulder."

"Yes, ma'am." One corner of his mouth lifted in an amused and very compelling grin.

Caitlin's heart fluttered. No doubt about it, the attraction hadn't died.

With the van unloaded, there was no reason for him to remain.

"Will I see you later?" she asked.

"Tomorrow, if you're here."

The thought shouldn't have appealed to her as much as it did. Ethan had hurt her. Terribly. She'd be wise to take care where he was concerned.

Even so, a sweet rush of anticipation cascaded through her.

"I'm sure Clay can do without you training his horses for a couple of days."

"Probably." Ethan buttoned his denim jacket. "I'm the one who can't do without the practicing."

"Practicing for what?"

"The jackpot."

She stared at him blankly. "You're not competing."

"I am. Or I will be if I can last a full eight seconds at least once before then. Clay won't let me enter otherwise."

"Is that how you fell tonight? Bull riding?"

"No, saddle bronc."

"Are you crazy?"

"A little, I suppose," he said jokingly.

"More than a little." She started to remind him that he had only one good leg, then stopped herself. "Bronc riding is dangerous. I really wish you'd reconsider."

"Not a chance." He turned to go, then paused. "I'm glad you're home, Caitlin."

A few minutes ago, such a statement would have elicited a breathy sigh from her, foolish though it may have been.

Not now.

He was saddle bronc riding again. With a prosthetic leg! Why didn't he just jump off a three-story building? The results would be the same.

Caitlin had cheered Ethan on from the sidelines all those years ago. She'd also encouraged him the same way she'd encouraged her brother. Winning competitions required a certain amount of risk, after all.

She'd learned too late that taking risks came with a steep price. In her case, her brother, Justin, was the one to pay.

It would be no different for Ethan, and she refused to be there when he injured himself.

Except, as the on-site emergency medical personnel for the Duvall Rodeo Arena, she most likely would be the one to treat him.

Chapter Two

Ethan hated to admit it, but Caitlin was right. His shoulder hurt like a son of a bitch. It had all night, affecting his sleep, his ability to dress himself and his mood.

What if he really had torn something? Then he wouldn't be able to enter the jackpot, that was for sure.

The idea of going to the doctor and getting an X-ray wasn't quite as distasteful to him as it had been the night before. Maybe he could go to the urgent-care clinic. If he was lucky, he might run into Caitlin again.

He no sooner had the thought than he dismissed it. More likely than not she was married or in a committed relationship. Of course, finding out wouldn't be all that hard.

And if she was single, then what?

He doubted she'd go out with him, not after the way he'd dumped her with hardly a word. Then there was the matter of his leg—or lack of it. Beautiful, desirable women like Caitlin Carmichael didn't date men with missing limbs.

Gritting his teeth, he shoved his arms through the sleeves of his undershirt and tried to pull it over his head. He didn't get far. The pain immobilized him.

The next instant a knock sounded.

"What?" he hollered, his breathing labored.

The front door opened and his brother came in. "Good

morning to you, too." He stopped midstep and eyed Ethan curiously. "Having a problem?"

Ethan muttered to himself, not pleased at having an audience.

"What did you say?"

"I hurt my shoulder last night."

"Breaking one of Clay's horses?"

"A bronc trying to break me."

"Ah." Gavin wandered toward the newly remodeled kitchen. "Any coffee?"

"There's instant in the cupboard."

"Instant?" He grimaced.

"Beggars can't be choosers."

Ethan didn't particularly like instant, either. But he'd discovered since living alone the last few weeks that brewing a pot of coffee was a waste when he drank only one cup.

He and Gavin and their dad had resided comfortably in the main house for over a year. When Gavin's daughter, Cassie, moved in with them this past summer, they'd continued to get along. Soon, however, Gavin's fiancée, Sage, and her young daughter, Isa, would be joining the family permanently, and that was a little too much closeness for Ethan.

The old bunkhouse had seemed a good solution. Converting it into an apartment was taking time, though, and living amid the chaos of construction did get tedious. But Ethan didn't mind.

After a lifetime of cohabitating with others, including a barracks full of marines, he quite liked his solitude. No snoring, music or loud TV disturbing his sleep. No having to wait for someone to finish in the bathroom. No arguing about whose turn it was to wash the dishes or vacuum.

No one watching him put on his prosthetic leg, then turning away when he caught him staring.

"Want some?" Undeterred by the prospect of instant coffee, Gavin removed a mug from the cupboard.

"Naw. I already had my quota today." Readying himself, Ethan raised his arms, only to hesitate.

What was wrong with him? He'd endured far worse discomfort than this. The months following his accident—a nice, gentle euphemism for losing the bottom half of his leg in an explosion—had been a daily practice in pushing the boundaries of his endurance.

It hadn't stopped there. The first thing Ethan had done when he returned home was reveal his intentions to start training horses again, his job before enlisting. His family had tried to dissuade him, but eventually came to understand his reasons and the need that drove him.

Since no respectable cowboy wore athletic shoes when he rode, Ethan had used some of the money he'd saved during his enlistment to purchase two pairs of custom-made boots that fit his prosthesis. Within a few weeks, he was riding, and suffering a whole new kind of torturous pain. With determination, practice and continual exercise, he found the pain eventually lessened, though he still had his days.

He didn't start breaking horses until a chance meeting with Clay Duvall. Over beers at the local bar, his old friend had listened while Ethan outlined his ambitions. Then he'd offered him a job. In addition to the arena, Clay owned and operated a rodeo stock business that specialized in bucking horses.

The idea of competing again hadn't occurred to Ethan until he'd watched the cowboys practicing at Clay's arena. What started as a vague longing quickly grew into a burning desire. Ethan was tired of people looking at him differently. Tired of their sympathetic smiles.

Once he started competing again, all that would change. Ignoring the pain, he pulled on his undershirt, then walked through the partially framed living room to the freshly painted bathroom, where he removed a bottle of ibuprofen from the medicine cabinet.

"You need a day off to rest up?" Gavin hollered from the kitchen.

"Hell, no."

Both Ethan and his father worked alongside Gavin. With only thirty of the family's original six hundred acres remaining in their possession, they'd turned their ranch into a public riding stable. Many Mustang Village residents boarded their horses, took riding lessons or went on guided trail rides at Powell Ranch.

In addition, they'd started the stud and breeding business last month, after capturing Prince, a wild mustang roaming the McDowell Mountains.

"Maybe you should take it easy today," Gavin suggested, when Ethan returned to the kitchen.

"Don't worry about me." He glowered at his brother. "What are you doing here, anyway?"

"Prince is off his feed. I'd like you to take a look at him before I call the vet."

"I will. Later."

"I was hoping you could do it first thing."

Ethan thought his brother babied the wild mustang too much. Then again, the future of their family business relied heavily on Prince and his ability to breed. While he'd successfully mated with several mares since his capture last month, it was still far too early to determine if any pregnancies had taken, much less what kind of foals he would produce.

Gavin studied him as Ethan downed the painkiller with a glass of water. "Have you considered seeing a doctor?"

"Caitlin told me the same thing."

That got his brother's attention. Instead of leaving, which

was Ethan's hope, Gavin pulled out a chair at the dining table, removed his hat and made himself at home.

Great.

"You saw her?" he asked.

"Last night. She's working for Clay, running his first-aid station."

"Interesting."

Gavin's expression reminded Ethan of their father and, he supposed, himself. The Powell men all looked enough alike that most people immediately recognized them as family.

"That's what I thought, too," Ethan said, recalling the shock he'd felt when he first saw Caitlin. "She also works mornings at the middle school and afternoons at the urgent-care clinic."

"Uh-huh."

His brother was sure taking the news in stride. Then it hit him. "You knew she was back, didn't you?"

"We met when Cassie sprained her ankle in gym class, and the school called me to come pick her up."

"That was weeks ago. And you're only now telling me?"

"Figured it wasn't my place."

Another thought occurred to Ethan. "Caitlin ask you not to tell me?"

"No. Nothing like that."

"Did my name even come up?"

"We really didn't have time to talk. She was busy, and Cassie was complaining about her ankle."

Ethan started pacing the kitchen. Caitlin had known he'd returned to Mustang Valley and hadn't bothered to look him up.

Did he really expect her to, after the way he'd treated her? Probably not. Change that to hell, no.

"Look," Gavin continued, "it just slipped my mind. I had

a lot going on at the time. Capturing Prince. Starting the stud and breeding business. Sage and I getting engaged."

"Right," Ethan answered testily. He'd bet the entire contents of his wallet that running into Caitlin hadn't slipped his brother's mind. "I'm a big boy, bro. You don't have to watch out for me."

"Sorry. Old habits are hard to break."

Not exactly an admission, but close.

"Answer me this," Gavin said. "What would you have done if I told you she was back in town?"

"Apologize, for one." Which, now that he thought about it, wasn't something he'd done last night. "And make amends... if possible." He owed her that much.

"You going to ask her out?"

"Are you kidding?"

"Why not?"

"Even if I did, she'd turn me down flat. Besides, she's probably married by now."

"She isn't."

Ethan stopped pacing. "How do you know?"

"The subject came up."

"I thought you said you didn't have much time to talk to her."

"Doesn't take long to say, 'Hey, you ever get married?'"

Ethan groaned.

"What are you so mad about, anyway?"

Before he could reply, another knock sounded at the door.

"What now?" He stormed over and yanked the door open.

Clay stood on the other side. "You're in a fine mood." Without waiting for an invitation, he stepped inside. "I just came from Prince's paddock. He hasn't touched his food."

"We're heading there now," Ethan grumbled, snatching his jacket off the back of the couch where he'd left it.

"Any more of that coffee left?"

"It's instant," Gavin complained from his seat at the table.

Clay drew back in surprise. "Don't you have a coffee-maker?"

Ethan glared at him. "Don't you?"

Clay glared back. "What's bugging you?"

"He's mad that I didn't tell him Caitlin was working at the school." Gavin rose from the table.

"Can we not discuss this?" Ethan headed for the door.

"You going to invite her out?"

He ignored Clay's question.

"I already asked him that." Gavin went to the sink and deposited his mug. "He says no."

Annoyed, Ethan shoved an arm into the sleeve of his jacket, then swore loudly when his entire left side seized with fresh pain.

"How's the shoulder?" Clay asked.

"Fine." Ethan opened the door and stepped out onto the porch.

Clay came up behind him. "You don't act like it's fine."

"I'll be all right."

"What did Caitlin say last night?"

"Ice the shoulder and take ibuprofen. I've done both."

"Did she tell you to see a doctor?"

"I don't need to see a doctor."

"Don't believe him." Gavin joined them on the porch, shutting the door behind him. "He's hurting."

Ethan anchored his hat to his head as a strong gust of wind swept past them on its way down the mountain to the valley.

"See a doctor," Clay ordered. "Until you do, and until you're cleared, no bronc riding."

Ethan swung around. "Dammit, Clay!"

"Sorry. That's the rule. Same for you as everyone else."

"The jackpot is a week and a half away. I need to practice."

"Then I guess you'd better haul your butt to the doctor today."

AT THE BOTTOM OF THE LONG driveway leading from Powell Ranch to the main road, Ethan turned left. Three minutes later he reached the entrance to Mustang Village, with its large monument sign flanked by a life-size bronze statue of a rearing horse.

As he drove at a reduced speed through the equine-friendly community, he tried to remember what it had been like when there were no houses or buildings or people, only wide-open spaces and Powell cattle roaming them. He'd missed out on the construction of the community, having been in the service at the time. How hard it must have been for his father and brother to watch their family's hundred-year-old history disappear acre by acre, replaced with roads, houses, condos and commercial buildings.

He generally avoided Mustang Village. The reminder of all they had lost was too hard on his heart.

If not for his mother's failing health, they wouldn't have borrowed the money from Clay's father and used their land as collateral. If Clay's dad had honored the agreement and not sold the land out from under them, Mustang Village would never have been built. If not for the residents of Mustang Village, Ethan's family would be raising cattle rather than operating a riding stable.

A lot of ifs, and that wasn't even counting the most recent one—if he hadn't been standing where he was at the exact moment the car bomb exploded, he wouldn't have lost his leg.

Ethan turned his thoughts away from the past when Mustang Village's one and only retail strip center came into view. It always struck him as odd to see hitching rails and bridle paths in a residential community. On any given weekend, there were almost as many equestrians riding about as there were pedestrians walking. Not so much during the week. Mustang Village resembled most other communities then, with school buses making runs, mothers pushing strollers, cyclists zipping along and dog lovers walking their pets.

Today, a work crew was busy stringing Christmas lights along the storefronts and hanging wreaths on lampposts. Already? Thanksgiving was still more than a week away.

A buzzer announced Ethan's arrival at the urgent-care clinic. This was his first visit. He always drove to the VA hospital in Phoenix for his few medical needs.

Inside the crowded clinic, a receptionist greeted him with a friendly "May I help you?" and handed him a clipboard. When he was done filling out the forms, she processed his co-pay and said, "Have a seat."

Ethan considered inquiring if Caitlin was working. But then the phone rang, followed immediately by a second line ringing. He left the receptionist to answer her calls, and sat in a chair next to a mother and her sniffling child.

He couldn't help thinking that if the bronc hadn't thrown him last night, he wouldn't be here now, anxiously waiting to see his former girlfriend again. Yet another if in a long, long list of them.

Except Ethan really wouldn't describe Caitlin as a girlfriend. She'd been much more than that to him, and he to her. Had his mother not died and he not enlisted, chances were good they'd have gotten married.

He really had to stop thinking about what might have been, or else he'd drive himself crazy.

"Ethan?"

His head snapped up when Caitlin called his name. "Yeah."

"Right this way."

He followed her down the corridor. Once he was weighed and his height taken, she escorted him to an examination room, where he sat on the table and she at the computer terminal.

"Why are you here today?"

Seriously? She knew darn well why. "I fell from a horse last night and hurt my shoulder," he answered, playing along.

"What part of your shoulder?"

"You examined me."

She gave him a very professional smile. "It's procedure."

He cupped his shoulder with his palm.

More questions followed, and she typed the answers into the computer. During the entire process, Caitlin treated him like any other patient, concerned, interested and like they hardly knew each other.

What did he expect? She was at work.

What did he want?

The answer was easy. To see that light in her eyes.

"The doctor will be right in to see you." Before closing the door, she smiled and said, "I'm glad you came in today."

He was tempted to jump to the wrong conclusion and reminded himself that her remark was medically motivated. Hadn't she urged him last night to have his shoulder looked at?

After a brief consultation with the doctor, Ethan waited again, this time for the X-ray technician. Returning from the imaging room, he waited a third time.

The doctor's news was good. Nothing was torn, only soft-tissue damage.

"Can I start riding again right away?" he asked.

"I recommend you take a few days off." The man studied him over a pair of reading glasses. "A week would be better."

"But there's no reason I can't ride."

"You could sustain further injury."

"Okay." Ethan nodded. He had every intention of getting on a bronc tonight, and he was pretty sure the doctor knew it.

"I'm going to prescribe an anti-inflammatory and a muscle relaxant. If you aren't better in two weeks, call for a follow-up exam or see your regular doctor."

"Thanks."

"You know—" the man removed his reading glasses "—if you're really that determined to ride, you might consider physical therapy to speed your recovery."

"Appreciate the advice, Doc."

"The nurse will be in shortly with your prescriptions."

Another wait, this one not long. Caitlin returned with three slips of paper in her hand. Ethan had to admit the sight of her in pale green scrubs was as surreal as seeing her in sweats. In college, she'd majored in journalism, with ambitions of being a TV reporter, and always dressed fashionably.

Admittedly, the scrubs looked cute on her, the loose material not quite hiding her very nice curves.

"Here you go." She handed him the prescriptions. "The doctor wrote one for physical therapy as well, in case you need something for the VA."

"I'll probably skip PT."

"Why? It will help."

He stood, folded the prescriptions and placed them in his wallet. "The nearby facilities don't take VA insurance. And I can't afford the time off work to drive into Phoenix."

"What if…what if I provided your physical therapy?"

"You?"

"I have some basic training. I'm not licensed, but I've taken several classes. For Justin. During his rehab, he'd strain his upper body muscles. And now that he's involved in wheelchair athletics, he's always overdoing it."

"I can relate."

"You two are alike when it comes to that." Her expression softened, and suddenly she was the seventeen-year-old transfer student who'd been assigned to sit next to him in calculus class.

Ethan was caught off guard and needed a moment to collect himself. "I don't think the VA will pay for a private physical therapist."

"I won't charge you."

He shook his head. "I can't ask you to do it for free."

"Who said anything about free?" She smiled then, *really* smiled, and he caught another glimpse of the confident, carefree girl he'd fallen in love with. "I was hoping we could negotiate a trade."

She had his attention now. "I'm listening."

She motioned him into the hall.

"I'm on the Holly Days Festival committee," she said.

The residents of Mustang Village had put on a big community-wide event the previous Christmas. None of the Powells had attended, but they'd heard about it. From everyone.

"The committee, huh?"

"You know me."

He did. She'd been an involved student in both high school and college. Cocaptain of the cheerleading squad, student council, National Honor Society.

"I thought the festival was strictly for residents."

"I'm a resident," she said brightly as they entered the reception area.

"Really?"

"I'm renting a condo. In the complex right across the street." She nodded toward the window. "I get to walk to work every day. Well, not to the middle school. But here."

Working *and* living in Mustang Village. Was that another

bit of interesting information Gavin had conveniently forgotten to tell Ethan?

"The committee is hoping to try something different this year," Caitlin went on. "The parade was fun, but more people participated than watched."

"You saw it?"

"I did. I almost drove to the ranch, too."

Just how often *had* they narrowly missed crossing paths since his return home?

"Anyway, I remembered that old farm wagon of yours and was wondering if we could decorate it and have you drive people around the park."

"No one's used that wagon in years."

Her hopeful smile fell. "Well, it was just an idea."

Ethan had no desire to participate in the Holly Days Festival. Nothing involving Mustang Village appealed to him—with the exception of Caitlin. And she appealed to him far too much for his own good.

But hadn't he just told Gavin this morning that he wished he could make amends with Caitlin? Wagon rides at the festival wouldn't exactly clean the slate. But it was a start, and obviously important to her.

"We could pull the wagon out of storage," he said. "See what kind of shape it's in."

"Great!" Her green eyes lit up.

This was the moment Ethan had been waiting for, only her excitement was over an old wagon. Not him.

"Why don't you come out to the ranch?"

"When?"

Ethan massaged his left shoulder. "As soon as possible. I still haven't qualified for the jackpot next weekend."

"What about tomorrow, say around noon? I have a two-hour break between the school and the clinic. If the wagon is usable, we'll set up a schedule for your PT sessions."

"Sounds good."

"Hey, Caitlin." The receptionist held up a manila folder.

"I have to go," she said hurriedly. "Thank you, Ethan." She collected the folder and called the next person's name.

Once again, Ethan was just another patient—and it didn't set well with him.

Chapter Three

In days gone by, Caitlin would have driven directly to the main house at Powell Ranch and parked there. Instead, she followed the signs and went around behind the cattle barn to the designated parking area.

"It's weird," her brother said from beside her in the passenger seat. "The place is totally different, but not different."

"Yeah, weird." She opened her door and stepped out.

Memories that had hovered the last few days promptly assailed her. Most were good, gently stroking emotional chords. One wasn't so good, and it quickly overpowered the rest.

"When was the last time you were here?" Justin asked, already maneuvering his legs into position.

"Oh, about nine years ago."

Nine years, four months and...she mentally calculated... eighteen days. Not that she was keeping track.

She'd arrived that last evening intending to join the Powells for dinner, something she often did in the past. Even before the meal was served, Ethan took her out to the front courtyard and sprang the news on her. He'd enlisted. Signed up a week after his mother's funeral. A rather important decision he hadn't even bothered discussing with Caitlin.

A fresh wave of hurt and anger unbalanced her now, and she paused, holding on to the van door for support.

Guess she hadn't moved past her and Ethan's bitter breakup, after all.

It must be seeing the ranch again. Or seeing *him* again—for the third day in a row.

Enough is enough, she told herself. She could manage working with Ethan, seeing him at the clinic, administering his physical therapy. He was nothing more than her patient.

With actions honed from much practice, she removed her brother's wheelchair from the rear of the minivan and carried it to the passenger side, where he waited.

She'd have set the wheelchair up for him, except he insisted on performing the task himself. Rather than argue, she gave in. Being independent was important to Justin, and she respected his wishes even though her instinct was to do everything for him.

After hoisting himself into the wheelchair, he and Caitlin made their way to the stables. She figured the office was as good a place as any to start looking for Ethan.

"Sure are a lot of people here," Justin commented, rolling his wheelchair along beside her.

A half-dozen riders were gathered in the open area near the stables. Several more were in the arena, riding alone or in pairs. One enthusiastic mother clapped while her preschooler trotted a shaggy pony in circles.

"I hear it's even busier when school lets out for the day." Caitlin remembered when the only people on the ranch were the Powells and the cowboys who worked for them.

"I'll wait here," Justin said when they reached the small porch outside the office.

He could easily maneuver the three steps leading onto it, but he probably wanted to give Caitlin and Ethan some privacy.

Easing open the door, she stepped tentatively inside the

office. The sight of Ethan sitting with his back to her at an old metal desk gave her a start.

Not again, she chided herself. No more going weak in the knees every time she saw him.

Clearing her throat, she said, "Hello," then "Oh!" when the ancient chair swiveled around with a squeak.

The man wasn't Ethan.

"Hey." Gavin greeted her with a wide grin. "What brings you here?"

Caitlin vacillated between enormous relief and equally enormous disappointment. "I'm meeting Ethan."

"You are?"

Obviously he hadn't informed his family of her visit. She didn't know what to make of that.

"If he's not around—"

"He's here. Shoeing one of the horses."

"Is it all right if I interrupt him?"

"I'm thinking he won't mind."

Caitlin wavered, then blurted, "Can I ask a favor of you?"

"Sure."

"My brother's outside. Would you check on him for me? Without making it look like you're checking on him?"

"How's he doing?"

"Good. And he's perfectly capable of handling himself in new situations."

"But you worry."

"Constantly."

"Not a problem." Gavin's cell phone rang. "Let me take this call first."

"Thanks." Caitlin hurried across the office and out the door leading to the stables.

It was like stepping back in time.

The rich, familiar scents of horses and alfalfa filled her nostrils the moment she crossed the threshold. Daylight, pouring in from the large doorways on both ends of the long aisle, illuminated the interior better than any electric-powered lights could. Soft earth gave beneath her feet with each step she took. A barn cat dashed behind a barrel, then stuck its head out to peer warily at her.

Caitlin glanced around, her breath catching at the sight of Ethan not thirty feet away. He was bent over at the waist, the horse's rear hoof braced between his knees as he used a file to trim it.

How did he do that with a prosthetic leg?

How did he do that with a bad shoulder?

Fine, he was resilient. She appreciated that quality in an individual. Admired it. But shoeing a horse while injured was just plain stupid. So was bronc riding.

She started to say something, only to close her mouth when Ethan released the horse's hoof and straightened.

He stood tall, his blue work shirt rolled up at the sleeves and stretched taut across his muscled back. The leather chaps he wore sat low on his hips, emphasizing his athletic frame. She couldn't remember him ever looking better. Or sexier.

When they were in high school, Caitlin had liked him best in his football uniform. Next best in the tux he'd worn to their senior prom. She'd been the envy of every girl on the cheerleading squad, and had relished the attention.

What an idiot she'd been. Shallow and silly—placing too much importance on things that didn't matter.

Ethan turned, and she wished suddenly she was wearing nice clothes. Not an oversize hooded sweatshirt and scrubs.

"You made it."

"I did."

He set the file he'd been using down on a box of tools. Next, he removed his chaps and draped them over the box. "Ready to take a look at the wagon?"

"Is that Chico?" Caitlin advanced a step, then two. "Can I pet him?"

"Of course."

"I remember him. I can't believe he's still around." She stroked the old horse's soft nose, and he snorted contentedly.

"That's right. You and Chico are already acquainted."

Caitlin was never much of a horse enthusiast, though she'd tried her best to share that interest with Ethan. When they did go on a ride, Chico was her mount of choice.

"He's Isa's horse now."

"Isa?"

"Sage's daughter. Gavin's soon-to-be stepdaughter. She's six and in love with this old guy."

"I'm glad." Glad the horse Caitlin remembered with such fondness was adored by a little girl and that some things around Powell Ranch hadn't changed.

"Do you still ride?"

"No, not since Chico." She didn't want to admit to Ethan how much riding—or any physical activity that held risk—scared her. She hadn't been like that before Justin's accident. Quite the opposite.

"I'll take you sometime." Ethan moved closer.

Caitlin's guard instantly went up. She continued stroking Chico's nose in an attempt to disguise her nervousness—at Ethan's proximity and the prospect of getting on a horse again. "We should probably take a look at the wagon. I have to get to the clinic soon."

They left the stables. Chico, Ethan assured Caitlin, would be just fine tied to the hitching rail, and was probably already napping.

As they rounded the corner of the cattle barn, she noticed lumber stacked nearby, along with a table saw, ladder and toolboxes.

"What are you building?"

"We're converting the old barn into a mare motel for the stud and breeding business. Clay and his men are helping us."

Ethan took her elbow and guided her around more piles of construction material. She started to object and insist she was fine, then changed her mind. Like the other night when he'd insisted on unloading her medical supplies, it would be like arguing with a brick wall.

He led her to a corner of the barn where, behind a tower of wooden crates and beneath a canvas tarp, the wagon stood.

"Not sure we can get much closer," he said, stepping over a roll of rusted chicken wire.

Caitlin squeezed in behind him, acutely aware of his tall, broad frame mere inches from her.

He leaned over and lifted the tarp, revealing a wagon wheel. Without thinking, she reached out and touched the worn wood.

A memory of Ethan driving her around the ranch in the wagon suddenly surfaced, of her bouncing in the seat beside him and both of them laughing. How carefree they'd been back then.

She suddenly missed those days with a longing she hadn't felt in years.

Stop it!

Dwelling on that period of her life would do more damage than good. She and Ethan might have renewed their acquaintance, but that was all it was, an acquaintance. All it could be. Even if she finally got past the hurt he'd caused her, he rode saddle broncs for pleasure and broke green horses for a living. Caitlin wasn't capable of caring for someone who courted danger on a daily basis. Not after what had happened to her brother. She couldn't live with the constant worry and fear.

"Going to need a few repairs." Ethan wiggled a loose spoke.

Caitlin was relieved to get back on track. "And lots of cleaning."

"Hope you have enough volunteers."

She studied the wagon with a critical eye. "I might need more."

"I've been thinking. Would it be all right if we asked for a small donation? Completely voluntary, of course. Sage, my future sister-in-law, is starting a wild-mustang sanctuary here on the ranch, and she's having trouble obtaining funding."

"What a good idea. I can't imagine the festival committee having any objections."

"That'll make her happy."

Caitlin brushed dirt off the wheel. "When can we get started?"

"Saturday soon enough?"

"We'll have to be here early. I'm due at Clay's arena after lunch."

"Me, too."

"You're not riding!"

"Planning on it."

"Your shoulder!"

"I can't afford to miss any practices."

"Isn't it dangerous to ride with an injury? I'd think your reaction time would be slowed."

"I'll wrap it."

As if that would fix everything. His attitude was exactly the reason they would never date again, no matter how attractive she found him. Riding broncs was bad enough. Riding broncs with an injury was idiotic.

"I'll have a couple of the guys help me pull the wagon out," he said.

"I recommend you *supervise* a couple of the guys." She leveled a finger at him. "If you're going to ride on Saturday, you need to rest that shoulder and let it heal."

"Right."

He was impossible.

"I need to get going." She stepped over the roll of rusted chicken wire. "I don't want to leave Justin alone too long."

"You brought him with you?"

"He doesn't have class on Fridays and sometimes comes by for a visit."

"Justin drives?"

"A Honda Civic. Modified, of course."

"And he lives with your parents?"

"No, he has an apartment near campus with a roommate."

"Not that it's any of my business," Ethan said, "but if the kid lives on his own and drives, don't you think he'll be okay alone for a few minutes?"

She sighed with exasperation...at herself. "I can't help worrying about him. Call it big-sister-itis."

"His accident wasn't your fault."

Caitlin went still, swallowed a gasp. No one other than Justin and her parents knew of her guilt and the reason for it.

How in the world had Ethan guessed?

Stupid question. He'd always been able to read her better than anyone.

She averted her face, hiding the sudden storm of emotions churning inside her. Him, this place, the memories of happier times—it was all too much.

Ethan took her elbow again, helping her navigate the narrow path through the construction material. His fingers were warm and strong and far too familiar. Any hope Caitlin had for control flew out the window.

"You weren't at the river that day," he said, his voice gentle with understanding. "You couldn't possibly have been involved."

His compassion and sympathy were her undoing.

"I encouraged him to go," she admitted, her throat burning. "If he had stayed home, he wouldn't have landed on that rock and damaged his spinal cord."

"Come on. Name one senior at our school who didn't tube down the river and jump from the cliffs the week after graduation. It was a rite of passage."

"Justin didn't normally disobey our parents." As she had, she thought. "I told him he was eighteen and it was time he stopped acting like such a geek. I drove him to his friend's house, then lied to our folks about where he was going."

"Teenagers disobey their parents. It's what they do."

"Being popular was so important to me in high school. Justin was such a nerd back then. Shy and scrawny and brainy. He was practically invisible. I thought if he went tubing, he'd break out of his shell. Because of me, his life is ruined."

They came to a stop at the entrance to the barn. Ethan released her elbow, only to drape an arm around her shoulders.

"Trust me, you weren't the only one pressuring him to go tubing. His buddies were, too."

It would have been nice to lay her head on Ethan's chest as she'd done so often in the past, and let him comfort her.

She might have, if she wasn't convinced she'd be sending him the wrong message.

Wiping her eyes, she tried to ease away from his embrace. He'd have none of it.

"When someone's seriously injured, like Justin, it's pretty common for family members and friends to blame themselves. My dad and brother were the same way. Kept thinking if they'd been there for me when Mom was sick, and after she died, I wouldn't have enlisted and been caught in that explosion. Eventually, they came to accept it was my decision to join the marines, and rotten luck I was standing where I was that day. Same with Justin."

Caitlin looked up at Ethan. "You don't think I was there for you when your mom died?"

At the time, she'd been so embroiled in her own misery over his abrupt departure, she hadn't considered the reason he left was because of her. How incredibly selfish.

"What? Of course not. I was the one unable to cope with my grief, so was pushing people away." He inhaled deeply. "I'm sorry, Caitlin. For abandoning you like that."

"I appreciate the apology."

"I know it's not enough to make up for what I did to you."

"No, it isn't."

He drew back at her brutal, but honest, admission.

"You're not the only one who had to deal with traumatic events," she said. "I did, too. And believe me, there were plenty of times after Justin's accident when I wanted to run away and leave everything behind. But I didn't. I stayed and dealt with my responsibilities regardless of how difficult it was. I just wish you had loved me enough to do the same."

CAITLIN'S REMARK HIT ETHAN like a blow. How could she think he hadn't loved her enough? The whole reason he'd left was because he had loved her *too* much. She deserved more than a man who was emotionally devastated, out of work and whose family was financially ruined, thanks to one man's insatiable greed.

Before he could explain, Justin came wheeling toward them. Ethan was pleased to see the young man, even if his timing stank.

"Hey, there you are." He pushed his wheelchair forward, meeting up with Ethan and Caitlin outside the cattle barn. "How are you doing?"

"I'm good." Ethan shook his hand, which was sheathed in a worn leather glove with cutouts for his fingers.

"I was just talking to Gavin. He filled me in on all the changes round here."

"Lots of them. Some good, some bad."

"You miss the old days?"

No one had ever asked Ethan that. He took a moment to consider before answering. "I do sometimes. I miss the people, especially. My mom and sister." He glanced briefly at Caitlin. If she was aware of his unspoken inclusion of her, she didn't show it. "But all things considered, I can't complain."

"Me, either," Justin said, without the slightest trace of bitterness.

Ethan's respect for him grew by leaps and bounds. If Justin felt self-pity at losing the use of his legs, he certainly didn't wallow in it.

"You in a hurry to leave?" Justin maneuvered his wheelchair so that he faced Caitlin. "I was hoping Ethan could show us the mustang."

"I can't be late for work."

Justin checked his watch. "I thought you didn't have to be at the clinic until two."

"I like to arrive a little early."

She sounded eager to go.

Ethan wanted the chance to explain his real reason for enlisting and leaving her, and was determined to find the opportunity. "It won't take long. Prince's stall is just behind the barn."

Justin started wheeling in that direction. Ethan followed, as did Caitlin, her gait stiff and her steps slow.

If she so obviously didn't want to be with him, why had she come along?

"I have to warn you," he told Justin, "the way there's bumpy."

"Can't be any worse than hiking Squaw Peak."

"You've done that?"

"Five times. Four of them in my chair." Justin beamed, his geeky smile reminding Ethan of the undersize, asthmatic kid he'd known when he and Caitlin were dating.

The smile, however, was the only thing about him that was the same. Justin had acquired some serious muscle on his upper body.

"Why do you keep him so far from the other horses?" he asked, guiding his wheelchair down the rocky slope to Prince's pen like a pro.

"He's too wild and unpredictable." Ethan kept his eyes trained on the ground, watching out for potholes and rocks. What would cause another person to merely stumble could send him sprawling. "And being near the mares tends to… excite him, shall we say. Better he's off by himself."

Where to house Prince had been an issue when they'd captured him last month. Clay solved the problem by erecting a temporary covered pen near the back pasture.

"I've been wanting to see Prince ever since I watched your brother on the news."

Ethan chuckled. "You caught that, huh?"

"Are you kidding? He was all over the TV."

The media had gotten wind of Prince's capture; a horse living wild in a ninety-thousand-acre urban preserve was big news. Several local stations had dispatched reporters to interview Gavin. The attention had resulted in a slew of new customers, giving the Powells' dire finances a much-needed boost.

"Watch yourself," Ethan cautioned as they drew near. "Prince is wary of strangers. He still doesn't like me and Gavin that much."

Justin showed no fear and wheeled close. Caitlin reached for his wheelchair as if she wanted to pull him back. After a second, she let her hand drop, though it remained clenched in a fist.

Was it only Justin's fall that had made her overprotective?

As they watched Prince, the stallion raised his head and stared at them. Then, tossing his jet-black mane, he trotted from one end of the pen to the other, commanding their attention.

And he got it. Ethan couldn't wait to see the colts this magnificent horse produced.

"He's bigger than he looked on TV."

Ethan kept a careful eye on Justin, ready to run interference if he ventured too close to the pen. Caitlin, on the other hand, seemed content to observe from a safe distance.

"Have you ridden him yet?" It was the first she'd spoken since Justin joined them outside the barn.

"No. He's only halter broke, and barely that."

"But you are going to break him?" Justin asked.

"Oh, yeah. My goal is by Christmas."

"That doesn't give you much time."

"You're right. He and I are going to have to come to a new agreement soon about who's boss."

Prince pawed the ground impatiently, as if daring Ethan to try.

Justin grinned sheepishly. "Don't suppose there's a horse in that stable of yours I could ride."

"Anytime you want, buddy." Ethan immediately thought of old Chico. If he was trustworthy enough for a six-year-old, he'd do fine for Justin. "Give me a call. I'll take you on a trail ride."

Beside him, Caitlin visibly stiffened. "Justin, are you sure about that? You've never had an interest in riding horses before."

"I never played sports before, either." He slapped the arm of his wheelchair. "Turns out I'm pretty good."

"What do you like?" Ethan asked.

"Basketball. Baseball. Swimming. I'm considering taking up track and field."

"I'm impressed."

"Well, I couldn't do any of it without Caitlin's help. She's amazing."

Did Caitlin pay for her brother's athletic expenses? Ethan wondered. That would explain the three jobs and why she worked fifty to sixty hours a week.

"You'll do fine at riding, then," he assured him.

Caitlin removed her cell phone from her sweatshirt pocket and checked the display. "It's getting late."

After a last look at Prince, the three of them returned to the stables, Justin chatting enthusiastically about riding and Caitlin stubbornly silent.

When they reached her minivan, Justin hoisted himself into the front passenger seat.

"I'll get that," Ethan offered, and carried the wheelchair to the rear of the minivan, where Caitlin had the hatch open.

She closed it the second he'd stowed the chair. "See you Saturday."

"What about physical therapy?" If he was keeping his end of the bargain, she needed to keep hers. "I'd like to start right away."

"I don't get off at the clinic until seven-thirty most nights."

"Eight's fine," he said, ignoring her attempts to postpone. "If it's not too late for you." He rose at the crack of dawn and assumed she did, too, what with her schedule.

"No, eight's okay." She peered nervously at her brother, who was busy with his MP3 player. "We can start tonight."

"Anything special I should have on hand?"

"I'll bring my portable table. We can set up just about anywhere."

"Okay. Drive straight to the bunkhouse and park there."

"The bunkhouse?"

"I live there now. Moved out of the main house so Sage and Isa can move in."

"O...kay."

"If you don't want to be alone with me—"

"It makes no difference," she answered tersely.

Somehow, Ethan thought it did. He just wasn't sure why.

Chapter Four

"Easy, boy." Ethan held on to Prince's lead rope, gripping it securely beneath the halter. "That's right, there you go." He ran his other hand down the horse's neck, over his withers and across his back, applying just the slightest amount of pressure. Prince stood, though not quietly. He bobbed his head and swished his tail nervously.

On the ground beside Ethan lay a saddle blanket, which he hoped Prince would allow to be placed on his back. The step was a small but important one toward breaking the horse. If Caitlin arrived on time, she'd be able to watch him.

He resisted pulling out his cell phone and viewing the display. It was 8:18. He knew this because he'd checked the time four minutes ago when it was 8:14, and every few minutes before that for the last half hour. He doubted she was going to keep their physical-therapy appointment, not after the disagreement they'd had this afternoon.

"Uncle Ethan!" Cassie yelled. "What are you doing?" She and Isa came bounding toward the round pen.

The horse's reaction to the girls' approach was immediate. Prancing sideways, Prince tried to jerk free of Ethan's hold...and almost succeeded.

"Relax, buddy," Ethan soothed, his grip on the lead rope like iron. Luckily, he was using his right hand. Thanks to the way his shoulder felt tonight, his left arm was pretty much useless.

The mustang, eyes wide, stared at Cassie and Isa, who peered at him and Ethan from between the rails of the pen.

"You girls stay back, you hear me? And keep ahold of that pup. I don't want him getting kicked."

They complied, sort of, by retreating maybe six inches. Cassie did scoop up her puppy, Blue, a five-month-old cattle dog mix that was out of her sight only when she was at school or a friend's house.

"Gonna ride him, Uncle Ethan?" Isa asked.

Though not officially a member of the family yet, Sage's daughter had already started calling Ethan "uncle." Probably because Cassie did. Isa copied the older girl's every move.

Ethan didn't mind. In fact, he rather enjoyed the moniker—and his role of the younger bachelor uncle who constantly set a bad example for his nieces by swearing in front of them and periodically losing his temper.

Months of counseling after the car bomb explosion had taught Ethan how to deal with his sometimes volatile and erratic emotions. Normally, he did a good job. On occasion, like earlier today, he wondered if maybe he'd quit attending counseling too soon, and should call the VA hospital for a referral. His buttons lay close to the surface and were easily pushed.

"Not tonight," he said, answering Isa's question. "Prince isn't ready."

"When *will* you ride him?" Cassie asked.

"Soon."

"That's what you said yesterday."

"Don't you girls have any homework?"

"We did it already," Isa volunteered.

"A TV show you want to watch?"

"We're still grounded until tomorrow," Cassie answered glumly.

"You're lucky that's all the punishment you got. If I'd pulled a stunt like you two did when I was a kid, Grandpa Wayne would have had me cleaning stalls every day before school and mucking out the calf pens."

Come to think of it, those had always been his chores. Both he and Gavin had helped their father and grandfather with the cattle business from the time they were Isa's age.

"Yeah, but if not for us, you wouldn't have captured Prince."

Cassie was right, even if her assessment of the situation was a mite skewed.

Last month, in an act of rebellion, she and Isa had taken off on horseback into the mountains without telling anyone where they were going. After a frantic two-hour search, they were found in the box canyon, along with Sage's missing mare and Prince.

The wild mustang had proved difficult to capture, requiring all of Ethan's and Gavin's skills as cowboys. It had also been one of the most exciting moments of their lives.

"Maybe not that night, but we'd have captured him eventually." Ethan continued stroking Prince, running his hand over the horse's back and along his rump. The movement aggravated the pain in his shoulder, but he ignored it.

"Did you ride a bronc earlier at Mr. Duvall's?" Cassie asked.

"I did." Ethan had gotten back to the ranch at seven and taken a quick shower just in case Caitlin showed up. He'd decided to work with Prince, because he didn't want to appear as if he was waiting for her—which he was.

"Did you make it a whole eight seconds?"

"Not quite. Almost four." Which was double his last time.

"Did you get hurt again?"

Why did everyone assume he couldn't fall without injuring himself?

"No, I didn't." He had, however, eaten a whole bucketful of arena dirt when he'd hit the ground. He should have taken another turn on a different bronc, but he figured one wreck a night was about all his body could handle.

He slowly bent and reached for the saddle blanket near his feet.

"What are you doing now?" Cassie asked.

"Hopefully, getting Prince used to this."

His plan didn't work. Prince reacted to the blanket as if a swarm of hornets might fly out from behind it at any second.

Wherever Prince had come from, and it was still a mystery, he'd never known human touch. Gavin claimed the horse was a descendant of the wild mustangs that had roamed the valley till the 1940s. Ethan thought that was impossible, but had yet to come up with a better explanation.

"Why don't you try a carrot or an apple?" Isa suggested. "That's what Mama used to train her horse."

"Good idea. What say you girls run in the house and see what you can find in the refrigerator."

Isa lit up. "Okay!"

"Uncle Ethan." Cassie turned and craned her neck. "Someone's here."

He saw the headlights of an approaching vehicle seconds before he heard the sound of tires crunching on gravel.

Had Caitlin finally arrived?

Excitement coursed through him when he recognized the familiar outline of her minivan.

Taking his eyes off Prince proved to be a mistake. The horse—possibly out of affection, probably out of dislike—butted Ethan in the shoulder. His injured shoulder.

"Shit!"

"Uncle Ethan!" Isa slapped her hands over her mouth. "You're not supposed to swear in front of us."

Cassie, a little older and a little wiser than her soon-to-be stepsister, appeared unfazed by the use of a four-letter word. "They parked in front of the bunkhouse," she informed Ethan, her eyes glued to the vehicle.

He unclipped the lead rope from Prince. "It's okay. You girls can go inside now."

Cassie and Isa didn't budge. Not until the minivan door opened and Caitlin stepped out.

"It's Nurse Carmichael from school," Cassie said with a very adult interest. "What's she doing here?"

Ethan slipped through the round-pen gate, leaving Prince inside. "If you must know, she's helping me with my shoulder." He set the saddle blanket on an overturned bucket by the gate, well out of Prince's reach.

"How?"

"Giving me physical therapy."

"Now?" Cassie furrowed her brow in an impressive imitation of parental concern. "Isn't it kind of late?"

"Seriously, you two," Ethan chided. "Get inside."

Unfortunately, Caitlin spotted them across the open area and started in their direction.

"Come on." Cassie grabbed Isa's hand. "Let's go say hi to her."

Ethan had no choice but to let them run ahead. He did well riding horses and walking from place to place, but he hadn't quite mastered the fifty-yard dash in under ten seconds.

Just as well. The extra time allowed him to study Caitlin. She didn't look as upset as she had earlier today. That, or she was hiding behind her nurse facade.

A tactic, he began to suspect, she frequently employed to keep people—him specifically—at a distance.

No more, now that he was onto her.

CAITLIN WAS SUDDENLY surrounded on all sides. "Well, hello, there."

"Nurse Carmichael." Cassie smiled exuberantly, her arm slung around the younger girl. "This is my stepsister, Isa. Well, she's not my stepsister yet, but she will be soon. Her mom's marrying my dad."

"Hi." The little girl stuck out her hand, her enormous grin adorable despite two missing teeth.

"Nice to meet you, Isa." Caitlin shook Isa's hand while gently disengaging her pant leg from the puppy's fiercely clenched teeth. "I heard you've been riding my old horse."

"Chico?"

"Uh-huh. He and I were good pals a lot of years ago."

"My dad never told us that." Cassie appeared suitably impressed.

"He may not have remembered."

"I don't know. He's got a pretty good memory. He's always boring us with stories about when he was our age."

"Yeah," Isa agreed, imitating Cassie's tone. "Boring us."

"He's not the one who took me riding." Caitlin glanced up as Ethan joined them, a familiar fluttering in her middle. "Your uncle Ethan did."

"Oh," Cassie said, as if she suddenly understood everything. "I see."

"Isn't it time for you two to hit the sack?" Ethan came up behind the girls and patted them on the head.

"Do we have to?" Cassie complained.

"Do we have to?" Isa echoed, only whinier.

"Get yourselves inside. Whether or not you go to bed is up to your parents."

"Just when it was getting good," Cassie mumbled under her breath.

"What about Prince?" Isa asked.

"He's fine in the round pen. I'll put him away later."

"Uncle Ethan's breaking Prince," Cassie announced with pride.

"He told me." Caitlin sent him a silent reprimand. "Except he's not supposed to do anything that might hurt his shoulder."

"Like bronc riding? 'Cause he went to Mr. Duvall's earlier."

"Exactly like bronc riding."

Would he ever learn? Ever change?

And what if he did?

"Scoot," Ethan admonished the girls, his voice warm with affection. "You've gotten me in enough trouble for one night."

"I'm not sure you need any help," Caitlin admonished.

"Never did."

So true. And for much of that trouble, she'd been his cohort. How many times had they sneaked out together when they were supposed to be home in bed? Or skipped class to head to the river? Or risked being caught making love when her college roommate was due back any minute?

No sooner were the girls out of earshot, the puppy chasing gleefully after them, than Ethan said, "About this afternoon—"

"It's okay. Really." Caitlin didn't want to talk about it. Not tonight. Maybe not ever. "Water under the bridge."

"I did love you. More than anything."

Why did he have to say that? "If you don't mind, Ethan, I've had a long day."

That did the trick, and he shut up.

They walked the short distance to his bunkhouse. Caitlin wasn't sure what to expect, having never been inside before. It had always been occupied by two or three ranch hands when she and Ethan dated.

They stopped at her van for her duffel bag and the portable table, which Ethan insisted on carrying despite her protests.

"This is nice," she commented upon entering the modest stucco structure.

"There's still a lot of work to do."

She noticed the partially framed walls dividing the single large room into a living room, bedroom and hall, and the smell of fresh paint lingering in the air. "It's bigger than I thought it would be."

He leaned the portable table against the kitchen counter. "To be honest, I didn't think you'd come."

"Like you said before, we have an agreement. And I don't back out on agreements just because the other person says something I don't like or don't agree with."

"Me, either."

"Good." Caitlin lightened her tone. "Because the committee is really excited about the Holly Days wagon rides." She removed her jacket and reached into the duffel bag, more than ready to get down to business. "I usually start with some heat therapy."

"Shirt on or off?"

"A T-shirt's fine."

Without any hesitation, he stripped off his denim jacket and work shirt and tossed them onto the couch.

Oh, boy. Clearly, she should have better prepared herself on the drive over. Whoever thought plain white T-shirts could be so sexy?

Tearing her gaze away required effort. She looked at his feet. "You might want to change out of those boots." Then she remembered his prosthesis. "But it isn't necessary."

"Be right back."

He stepped through the partially framed wall into the bedroom. Sitting with his back to her on the corner of the bed, he removed his boots. She thought she heard the sound of a zipper.

Rather than stare, she busied herself setting up the portable table and warming a hot pack in the microwave.

Ethan returned a few minutes later wearing a pair of athletic shoes.

"Have a seat." She indicated the kitchen chair she'd pulled out. "I brought these for tonight." She touched the pair of two-pound hand weights she'd set on the table. "Do you by chance have any of your own?"

"Not here. There might be some in the storeroom. It's been a while since I've worked out."

Caitlin remembered when Ethan had played football and basketball. While he'd lifted weights in the garage, she'd kept him company, talking and flirting and doing her best to distract him. Most of the time, it hadn't worked. But there were times it had....

Removing the hot pack from the microwave, she tested the temperature before laying it on his shoulder. Next, she busied herself readying the portable table. In truth, there wasn't much to do. She wiped it down twice with disinfectant spray just to avoid standing around. Ethan, she was sure, would attempt to fill the lull with conversation of a personal nature, and she was determined to keep their session completely professional.

"Is Justin the reason you became a nurse?"

Caitlin had been fluffing a small travel pillow. At Ethan's question, she set it down. Usually when people asked, she answered that she'd always wanted to be a nurse. Ethan, however, knew better.

"Yes." She smoothed the last remaining wrinkles from the pillowcase. "After the accident, I took an active role in his care. Found out I could actually stand the sight of blood. I'm a pretty good nurse. Who'd have guessed?"

"Me."

"Right." She gave a small laugh. "The last thing I was interested in when we were going together was taking care of other people."

"You're a softie. The first to jump in when someone needs assistance. Of any kind. I always figured you'd work in a people-oriented field."

What had Ethan seen in her all those years ago that she hadn't seen herself?

"Let's start on those exercises," she said briskly.

She spent the next twenty minutes showing him several simple exercises designed to loosen his muscles, build strength, decrease pain and restore mobility. Some of the exercises were done with weights, others without. Some standing, some sitting. When they were finished, Caitlin instructed him to lie on the table.

"Face up or down?" he asked.

"Up."

She thought she'd prepared herself for this part of the session. Once again, she was wrong.

Bending over Ethan, she wrapped her arms around his upper body, leaning in so that their faces were inches apart. Their positions, and the ones that followed, sorely tested her ability to remain detached. His dark eyes locked with hers. His chest rose and fell with each breath he took. His masculine scent filled her nostrils and triggered an onslaught of sensual memories.

The cheerfulness he'd exhibited earlier slowly vanished, and his features went from animated to stoic to strained. He, too, was being affected by their close proximity.

Levering a hand beneath his shoulder, she lifted his arm over his head, stretching it as far as his constricted muscles would allow. Unable to stop herself, she looked down at his face, bracing herself for the jolt of awareness that would race through her.

It didn't happen quite like she imagined.

Ethan tensed, his upper body involuntarily lifting several inches off the table. "Son of a bitch! That hurts."

"Sorry." Caitlin immediately relaxed her grip. "I didn't realize.... Justin usually lets me know right away when I'm pushing him too hard."

"That'll teach me to tough it out." Perspiration beaded his brow.

"Yes, it will." She kneaded his shoulder, noting when the tension ebbed away. "I really didn't mean to hurt you."

"You sure? I was thinking it was your way of getting back at me for all the misery I caused you."

"You *are* joking, right?" When he didn't reply, she said, "Ethan!"

"Yes. I'm joking."

His words didn't reassure her.

"Caitlin." He reached for her hand and clasped it in his.

She made a token effort to pull away, then gave up. Seeing him on the table, knowing he was in pain, tugged on that soft spot in her heart he'd talked about earlier.

All at once, he sat up and swung his legs over the side of the table.

"Wait," she protested. "We're not done."

"No, we're not."

It took her a second to realize he wasn't referring to their physical-therapy session.

"You misunderstood me." She tried to back away.

He gripped her hand, holding her firmly in place. "I want to see you again. And not just for more PT or when you and your crew are here working on the wagon."

"Ethan, we can't. I can't."

"Give us a chance."

"It's impossible."

"I know you haven't forgiven me yet."

"I'm working on it."

"Is it my leg?"

"God, no! That doesn't matter to me in the slightest." Despite her vehement objection, she could see by his expression he didn't believe her. "It's your bronc riding. And breaking horses for Clay. And the mustang. And telling Justin he can come here and ride anytime he wants."

"Why can't he?"

"It's too dangerous."

"Probably no more dangerous than basketball or baseball. Especially on old Chico."

"He could fall."

"He could have tipped his wheelchair on the way to see Prince."

"That's different, and you know it."

"I wouldn't put him on any horse that wasn't dead broke. And we have safety equipment if he wants. Helmets. A harness."

"It's not that. Justin gets enthusiastic. Tries to do more than he can."

"Don't you think he's the best judge of his limitations?"

She frowned. "I should have figured you wouldn't understand."

"You're wrong. I understand your brother very well. A whole lot better than you do, I'm guessing."

"That's not what I mean."

"A guy being disabled doesn't give other people the right to run someone's life or make decisions for him. Not even family. No matter how good their intentions are or how guilty they feel."

She flinched as if struck.

"Caitlin." Ethan released her and pushed off the table,

landing on his feet. "I'm sorry. I get defensive sometimes. Shoot off my mouth."

"You take chances, Ethan." She squared her shoulders. "Big chances. Without the slightest fear. Justin does, too."

"There was a time you liked that about me."

Oh, she had. Very much. "But not anymore."

"Justin's accident wasn't your fault!"

"That's not true. He got hurt pulling a stupid stunt I convinced him to do." Reaching for the hot pack, she began packing her duffel bag. "When I first became a nurse, I trained in a trauma center. I thought it would help me better understand Justin's needs. You can't imagine the injuries I saw."

"Actually, I can. I spent two months in a military rehab center."

"Then you have to understand where I'm coming from." She shoved item after item into the bag. "I lost count of how many people I treated who were victims of sport or recreational-related accidents. Skydiving, drag racing, skiing and, yes, horseback riding."

Ethan came up behind her. "People get hurt just walking across the street."

Damn. He was close. Too close. If he touched her, she'd give in or break down or otherwise embarrass herself.

No, not happening. She was strong and could resist him and these feelings whirling out of control inside her.

"Fewer people get hurt walking across a street than they do jumping off a cliff into the river or riding a wild bronc." She paused, steeling her resolve. "I can't handle someone I care about being hurt. Or worse. Not again." Her voice warbled on the last two words.

"Does that mean you care about me?"

Not the response she was expecting. She zipped the duffel bag closed. "Of course I do."

"Would you go out with me if I wasn't riding broncs or breaking horses?"

"I don't know. Maybe."

"Okay." He grabbed his shirt and put it on, not bothering to button it.

Okay?

"Are you saying you'd quit bronc riding and breaking horses for me?"

He replied without missing a beat. "No. I don't believe people have the right to demand someone to give up their passion as a condition of the relationship. That's unfair. I wouldn't ask you to give up nursing, just like I wouldn't ask my brother to give up what's left of this ranch."

This time he gave her the response she'd expected to hear.

It also confirmed what she knew to be true. There was no chance for her and Ethan. Not as long as he cared more about what he wanted than he did about her.

Chapter Five

Ethan didn't think he'd ever seen Clay's rodeo arena so busy. At least forty men had shown up to practice for the jackpot next weekend. The majority of them were bull riders, the rest bronc riders. Family members or girlfriends tagged along, bringing ice chests and folding chairs and lap blankets to ward off the chill. Those who didn't gather around the lowered tailgates of their trucks sat in the bleachers observing the practice rounds with interest. Even more stood by or straddled the fences, chatting up the cowboys.

"What's with folks in these parts?" Conner asked, settling into a vacant spot on the fence alongside Ethan. "Don't they have anything better to do on a Friday night?"

"I was just thinking the same thing."

Like Clay, Conner had been Ethan's friend since grade school. Conner sometimes helped the Powells, leading trail rides and giving roping lessons. He'd also been with them on that night in the mountains when they'd captured Prince. Conner's regular job was systems analyst for a large manufacturing plant in Scottsdale, though no one would guess by his well-worn jeans, scuffed boots and weathered cowboy hat that he held two degrees, one in computer science and the other in business management.

"Your brother invited me for Thanksgiving dinner."

"You coming?"

"Can't, pal. Going to be at the folks'."

"Come over later for dessert if you want."

This Thanksgiving would mark the first holiday the Powells had celebrated since Ethan's mother died. Of course, Ethan hadn't been home for most of those Easters, Thanksgivings and Christmases. He was really looking forward to the dinner this year, brightened considerably by the addition of Cassie, Sage and Isa.

"Are you riding tonight?" Ethan asked as he watched the young man preparing to go next, studying his techniques and comparing them to his own. The kid was inexperienced but showed real potential. He might do well at the jackpot.

"Hell, no." Conner snorted. "I'm not about to risk scrambling my brain."

According to Caitlin, that was exactly what Ethan did on a regular basis.

"You used to like bronc riding. Bull riding, too."

"Yeah, before I grew up."

What did that say about Ethan?

His attention wandered to the makeshift first-aid station beneath the announcer's stand. Caitlin had arrived a half hour earlier, unloaded several boxes and grocery sacks, then disappeared inside. She had yet to emerge. He hoped she was simply busy and not avoiding him after their...what? Second disagreement?

He didn't much like the habit they'd fallen into of late.

"Something bothering you?" Conner asked.

"Just got a lot on my mind."

"Like qualifying for the jackpot?"

"Oh, I'm going to qualify. If not tonight, then tomorrow."

Ethan had put his name in about ten minutes before Conner arrived. He figured he had a little time before heading over to the chutes.

"Clay letting you practice with that bum shoulder?"

"It's better." And it was better. Marginally. He hadn't in-cluded that qualifier when he'd talked to Clay, however. "I have to go in for a follow-up exam before the jackpot."

Another chance to see Caitlin.

"Then what's with the scowl?" Conner asked.

Ethan decided he didn't care for old friends who knew him too well. "I did something stupid last night."

"What else is new?"

He drew back in mock offense. "That's a fine thing to say."

"And true." When Ethan remained silent, Conner burst into deep, rich laughter. "Come on. Fess up, buddy."

"I sort of asked Caitlin out."

"Sort of?" Conner's brows shot up.

"I might have suggested that she and I test the relation-ship waters."

"Relationship waters! Just how much Dr. Phil do you watch?"

"You're not helping."

"All right." He laughed again. "What did she say?"

"In a nutshell, no. Not so long as I'm riding broncs and breaking green horses."

"You going to quit?"

At that moment, Caitlin emerged from the first-aid station. Shielding her eyes from the bright floodlights, she scanned the arena and nearby stands. Ethan guessed she was search-ing for Clay. Her gaze lit on him momentarily. No sooner did his pulse skyrocket than she nonchalantly looked elsewhere.

"No, I'm not going to quit," he told Conner.

"Why not?"

"Hell, I've barely started again."

"Why continue? We all know you can do it."

There it was again, the reference to him having something to prove.

"Except I *haven't* done it. Not for eight seconds."

"Is bronc riding really that important?"

"It's not the bronc riding."

"What then?"

"I just want to be Ethan Powell again. Not Ethan Powell who lost his leg while serving in the Middle East."

"That isn't how people think of you."

"Not you, maybe. But everybody else does."

"When did you become a mind reader?"

Ethan ignored Conner. People who were physically whole didn't understand. Didn't notice the stares. Ethan noticed. There were at least a dozen individuals casting discreet glances in his direction this very moment. And if he possessed superhearing, he was sure he'd catch his name being mentioned in every conversation at some point during the night.

Conner rested his forearms on the fence and shifted his weight from one foot to the other. "What makes you sure everyone walks around thinking there goes Ethan Powell, the peg-legged cowboy?"

Conner was lucky they were such good friends. If not, Ethan wouldn't let him get away with that last remark, teasing or not.

"I don't know," Conner mused out loud. "If it were me, and a gal as pretty as Caitlin Carmichael asked me to give up something for her, I'd be inclined to oblige."

Ethan's attention zeroed in on Caitlin. She stood beside the announcer's booth, pushing a breeze-blown lock of hair back from her face. He liked the shorter cut, once he'd gotten past the initial shock. The strands curled attractively around her face in a way they hadn't before. She wore jeans tonight and, unlike all the other loose garments he'd seen her in, they fit her to perfection.

Conner nudged Ethan in the ribs. "Why don't you go over and talk to her."

"We didn't exactly part on good terms last night."

After his declaration, she'd hurriedly packed her things. Refusing his help, she'd carted the portable table out to the van and hightailed it off the ranch without so much as a backward glance.

Ethan had spent another restless night, this one less from shoulder pain and more from mentally kicking himself for being such a fool.

"Ethan Powell!" The young woman Clay had recruited to help out checked off Ethan's name on the clipboard she was holding. "On deck."

He pushed away from the fence. "Guess I'm up."

"You sure about this?" All trace of joking was gone from Conner's voice.

Ethan shot Caitlin another glance. No question this time, she was staring straight at him. Even at this distance, he could discern the worry on her face. Or was that pleading?

If he wanted to, he could turn around, walk away from the chutes and toward her. Show her he was willing to compromise in order to test those relationship waters he'd mentioned earlier.

But when he took that first step, it was in the direction of the chutes. He sensed her tracking him the entire way. He also sensed her disappointment.

It wasn't enough to make him change his mind. Not with the dozens of spectators also tracking him and waiting for him to fail, thinking maybe he'd lost a part of his mind in that explosion along with his leg.

As the big brute he was about to ride greeted him with bared teeth and flattened ears, Ethan began wondering the same thing.

CAITLIN WATCHED ETHAN amble over to the chutes, her agitation mounting with each step he took. She so wished he'd give up this stupid—make that insane—idea of riding broncs. What was the matter with him? With all men? They had some kind of ridiculous ambition to risk life and limb just to prove they were tough.

Without consciously planning it, she moved trancelike toward the arena fence. Ethan had disappeared behind the chutes, preparing for his turn. Just as she reached the railing, he reappeared. Scaling the fence, he straddled the top and waited, conversing with the cowboy beside him.

Caitlin's initial thought was how lucky that the first-aid station was fully stocked and operational. Her second one—she hoped to heck he didn't need it.

"Think he'll go a full eight seconds this time?"

"Don't know. I still can't believe he's trying. If anything goes wrong…jeez, he's already lost one leg."

The people next to Caitlin were discussing Ethan. She had to agree with the second man's opinion.

Ethan slowly lowered himself onto the bronc's back. Caitlin's stomach constricted into a tight fist of worry. He'd survived two other rides that she knew of, but not unscathed. It could be worse tonight.

Standing on tiptoe, she craned her neck to see over the high wall of the chute. The only thing visible was the crown of Ethan's tan Stetson.

All at once the gate next to Ethan's chute opened and a figure on horseback burst through it. The ride lasted a few harrowing seconds and ended with the cowboy sprawled on his back in the dirt, his chest visibly heaving. So was Caitlin's. The horse, kicking his hind legs, loped in a victory circle until the pickup men were able to safely herd him to the far side of the arena and through the exit gate.

Caitlin, hands on the railing, ready to bolt into the arena

if necessary, expelled a sigh of relief when the cowboy rolled over and clambered to his feet. The crowd rewarded him with a round of applause as he walked, then jogged to the gate in order that the next participant—Ethan?—could go. Thankfully, the cowboy didn't appear in need of any medical attention. But another man had earlier in the evening. He'd suffered a nasty gash on his chin when his face collided with his saddle horn.

Caitlin had advised him to take the rest of the week off from bronc riding. He hadn't heeded her advice, but instead had gone right out and put his name in again. Crazy.

Like Ethan.

How did these wives and girlfriends here tonight stand watching the men they loved without constantly breaking down? Caitlin couldn't do it.

The wrangler manning the gates pulled the center one open, scrambling out of the way as he did. All at once a large, dark-colored horse hurtled into the arena, all four feet off the ground and Ethan astride his back.

Caitlin understood very little about bronc riding, despite having watched Ethan a hundred times in years past. There was more, she knew, to a successful ride than just remaining in the saddle for eight seconds. Something to do with how high the horse bucked and how expertly the cowboy rode him.

Both seemed to be happening as she watched Ethan. The horse achieved tremendous height, humping his back into a tight arc while Ethan hung on and rode the tar out of him.

Eight seconds had never lasted so long. Caitlin vaguely registered the sound of a buzzer going off. As the pickup men flanked the horse, one of them grabbed the bucking strap and jerked it loose. The horse immediately stopped kicking and began trotting. The other pickup man extended his arm to Ethan, who reached for it.

Caitlin relaxed, let her shoulders sag. The worst was over.

Suddenly, the horse gave a last mighty buck and unseated Ethan, launching him into the air. Caitlin stifled a cry and clung to the fence railing with such force the coiled wire cable cut into her palms.

By some miracle, Ethan righted himself and landed on his feet…only to pitch face-first onto the ground. The crowd let out a collective gasp.

Caitlin found herself hurrying along the arena fence, stopping when she was directly across from the spot where he had fallen. The first pickup man rode his horse over to check on Ethan, blocking her view. She was just about to move when Ethan began to rise. The crowd applauded as he stood and hobbled awkwardly away.

Hobbled! Had he hurt his good leg? What would he do? How would he get around? He must be in terrible pain.

She followed him from the other side of the fence, zigzagging between people in an effort to keep up. She lost sight of him when he exited through the gate and had to make a detour around the cattle pens. By now, she was practically running.

Where had he gone?

Finally, thankfully, she located him standing behind the chutes, talking to a group of men. Hands braced on his hips, he leaned forward at the waist. It was a posture Caitlin often observed in people who were injured.

Enough was enough. She'd drag him, kicking and screaming if necessary, to the first-aid station and examine him. Keep him still long enough to listen to her advice to take it easy.

She set out, resolute. At the same moment, one of the men clapped Ethan on the back and laughed loudly. Caitlin was shocked. Did the cowboy have no consideration for someone in pain?

"Ethan," she called.

He turned then. And rather than a grimace, his face wore a wide, exuberant grin.

Sweet heaven, he was handsome. She came to an abrupt halt, her mind emptying of everyone and everything save him and what they'd once had together. What they could have together now if he would just come to his senses.

He limped toward her. "Did you see?"

"Yes. Are you all right?"

"I couldn't be better."

Realization dawned. Slowly, but it dawned. The men surrounding Ethan were congratulating him. Because he... She recalled hearing the buzzer. He had gone a full eight seconds. He'd said something about that the other night. If he lasted eight seconds, Clay would allow him to compete in the upcoming jackpot.

Dammit!

Fury bubbled up inside her. More at herself than Ethan. What a fool she'd been to think even for a few seconds that they could rekindle their former relationship.

"I just wanted to make sure you were okay."

She expected him to return to his friends. After all, her tone had been anything but inviting.

Only he didn't. He kept coming straight toward her. Before she could object, he hauled her into his arms and swung her in a wide circle.

"Put me down before you hurt yourself again."

"I did it!"

"Ethan, please. Your shoulder."

He released her. The moment her feet touched the ground, he lowered his mouth to hers, stopping a fraction of an inch shy of kissing her.

"I've been wanting to do this for the last three days."

Three days? Was that all?

She'd been waiting the past eight years, eleven months and twenty-one days to kiss him.

Just like that, their years apart melted away. Ethan's lips moved expertly over hers, applying just the right amount of pressure to coax a melting response from her. He'd always been an amazing kisser. That, or they were just amazing together. Their bodies fit perfectly. Her soft curves nestled against his hard planes as his arm circled her waist and drew her against him.

Caitlin was tempted to lose herself in his kiss. Set aside her worries and concerns and embrace the moment. And she did…until sanity returned, giving her a big, solid kick. The hoots and hollers of Ethan's cowboy friends might have had something to do with it, too.

Just how many people were watching them?

Caitlin broke off the kiss and pressed a hand to her flaming cheek. Ethan didn't appear the least bit embarrassed. Of course not.

"That shouldn't have happened," she stammered, and backed away.

Ethan started after her. "But it did happen," he said in a low voice. "And for a minute there, you were liking it every bit as much as I did."

Had they really kissed for more than a minute?

Wilting beneath stares from dozens of eyes, she executed a hasty retreat.

"Caitlin." Ethan appeared beside her.

"I don't want to talk." She couldn't. Her thoughts were in a jumble. She'd wind up saying something she'd regret. "Not now." She brushed past him.

"I need— Wait up, Caitlin!"

Through the haze of fog surrounding her, she heard the note of urgency in Ethan's voice. Still fuming, she almost didn't stop.

Almost.

She spun around just in time to see him crumple, a look of pure agony on his face.

"Ethan! Are you all right?" Instinct took over, and she ran to him. Dropping to her knees, she touched his head and back with gentle fingers. "What happened?"

He pushed himself to a sitting position. "I thought you were mad at me." Labored breathing punctuated each word.

"I am mad at you."

His grimace turned into a lopsided smile. "Then how come you didn't keep walking?"

"I'm a nurse."

"That's not why."

She made a sound of frustration. "Are you hurt or not?"

"It's my leg."

"Did you sprain it?"

"No." He groaned and shifted his weight.

Between their heated kiss and Ethan's fall, they'd drawn a sizable audience. Some of Ethan's friends expressed their concern and offered assistance.

"I'll be all right," he insisted. "My leg came loose in the fall."

His prosthesis. Thank goodness that was all.

Two of his buddies hauled Ethan upright. Still grinning, he slung an arm around their shoulders.

"Where to?" the taller of the pair asked.

"The first-aid station."

Caitlin hurried ahead of them to open the door and flip on the light. The men brought Ethan inside and deposited him in the same metal folding chair he'd sat in that first night.

"You need anything?" one friend asked.

"Naw, I'm fine." He nodded at them both. "Appreciate the lift."

The taller man tipped his hat at Caitlin and followed his buddy outside.

"What can I do?" she asked.

"I've got it." Ethan didn't exactly push her away, but he made it more than clear with his gesture and tone that he didn't want her hovering. Bracing his hands on the chair seat, he managed to stand, though unsteadily. His loose prosthesis hung at an odd angle in front of him.

She rushed forward, stopping short when he snapped, "I've got it!"

"Okay."

Patients often refused help. She had learned to navigate the fine line between respecting their wishes and providing the care they needed. She watched him intently from beside the table, ready to jump in if necessary.

With his free hand, he reached for his belt buckle and unfastened it with a flick of his wrist.

Her breath caught. "What are you doing?"

"Putting my leg back on."

Naturally. How silly of her.

In order to get at his prosthesis, he had to remove his pants. There was no other way.

What had she been thinking?

Once he had his jeans unzipped, he slid them down his hips and sat back in the chair. His shirttails covered him. Only the lower part of his blue—blue?—boxer shorts was visible. Caitlin averted her gaze, concentrating on his feet.

The prosthesis, caught in the pant leg, didn't cooperate. Without thinking, she knelt in front of him and grabbed it by the boot.

"You don't have to." Ethan's hands grappled with hers.

"Let me," she said softly. "Please."

She lifted her face to his. She could read in his eyes how

difficult this was for him. He didn't want people seeing him at his most vulnerable.

Gripping the hem, she pushed the prosthesis back up his pant leg.

Ethan didn't move at first. Then, taking hold of the prosthesis around the cup, he fitted it to his stump. There was a quiet whoosh as air escaped. When he was done, he secured the elastic cuff, which had slipped off during his fall.

She said nothing, knowing the more professional she acted, the easier it would be for Ethan. Easier for her, too.

As soon as he was done, they both stood. She placed a hand on his lower back to steady him while he pulled up his jeans and tucked in his shirt.

"Thank you," he said, buckling his belt.

"That's why I'm here, and what Clay pays me for."

"Is that the only reason?" He pinned her in place with those dark brown eyes of his.

If only she could lie. Say that helping him was just her job. Nothing more.

But her mouth refused to listen to her brain's instructions. What they'd just shared had in some ways been more intimate than their earlier kiss. To lie would be dishonoring that moment and the undeniable, yet impossible, connection they shared.

"No, Ethan. It's not the only reason." She straightened, set her mouth in a resolute line. "But we both know it should be."

Chapter Six

Ethan stood outside the round pen. He'd been up since five this morning, working with Prince. His deadline for breaking the mustang, as he'd told Justin the other day, was fast approaching, and he was determined to make some real progress. After two patience-testing hours, ones that aggravated his shoulder considerably, Ethan had the saddle blanket on Prince's back, along with a lightweight pack saddle.

Prince didn't like either, and alternately trotted and loped in circles as if he could outrun them. Each time he stopped, he glared menacingly at Ethan.

"Not yet, pal. A little while longer."

Prince stomped his left foot, then started trotting again.

Gavin came up beside Ethan. "I'm impressed."

"Don't be. The pack saddle may be on his back, but he's far from accepting it."

Prince came to an abrupt halt across from them. Reaching his head around, he took hold of the blanket with his teeth and gave an angry yank. Ethan imagined Prince trying that same move with his pant leg when he finally managed to mount the horse.

"You ready to help me with that wagon before Caitlin gets here?" he asked.

Gavin hitched his chin at Prince. "What are the chances

that blanket will be in shreds and the pack saddle in pieces when we get back?"

Prince was now sniffing the cinch holding the saddle in place, and making irritated snuffling sounds.

"I bet he'll quiet down the second we're gone," Ethan said.

"Hmm."

"He always has to put on a show. Let everyone know how tough he is."

"He's not the only one."

"Are you referring to me?" They set out in the direction of the old cattle barn.

"I heard about your fall last night."

"Did you also hear I qualified for the jackpot?"

"I did. And congratulations. So, how badly were you hurt?"

"My leg came loose is all."

"Is that why Caitlin kissed you?"

Now it was Ethan's turn to grin. "It was more the other way around. I kissed her."

"Clay said she didn't act like she objected."

"He was there?" Ethan scratched his head. "Really?" What else had he missed when all his attention was riveted on Caitlin?

"Am I to assume the two of you are back together?"

"No. She's made it pretty clear there's no chance of that."

"Then why the kiss?"

"I'd just finished my ride. And she looked really pretty. I couldn't help myself."

"Be careful you don't hurt her again."

Ethan had been having similar thoughts. But then he'd recall Caitlin's lips, soft and pliant and molding to his. She might be resisting him at every turn, but there was no denying her response.

She still cared, and the knowledge pleased Ethan enormously.

As far as what he'd felt when she'd helped him with his prosthesis, he still wasn't sure. Not since his last visit to the VA hospital had he allowed anyone to view his prosthesis up close, much less touch it. He could argue Caitlin was a nurse, but that wasn't the reason he'd accepted her help.

He trusted her. Simple as that. Unfortunately, she didn't trust him in return.

It was a situation he intended to rectify.

He and his brother spent ten minutes unburying the wagon, and another ten rearranging the surrounding junk, as Gavin called it. They were just rolling the wagon into the open area near the horse-bathing rack when Caitlin's minivan pulled up, an older model sedan following in its wake. Ethan was surprised to see Justin in the passenger seat of her van, considering she didn't want him anywhere near horses.

"Hi." She greeted Ethan and Gavin with a bright smile that revealed nothing other than her delight at finding the wagon ready for her crew of volunteers to clean, repair and decorate.

Introductions were made. Four helpers beside Justin had accompanied Caitlin—an older man, a middle-aged woman and a couple in their early twenties who were obviously boyfriend and girlfriend. That relationship didn't prevent Justin's gaze from constantly traveling to the young woman.

Poor guy. He looked on the verge of falling head over heels for a woman who was completely unavailable.

Ethan was no different.

"I'm going to check on Prince," Gavin said after a bit. "Nice to meet you all."

Ethan probably didn't need to hang around the volunteers, either, but he couldn't make himself leave.

The older man proved to be quite handy with a hammer,

wrench and electric drill. Together, he and Ethan repaired the broken wheel, cracked seat and loose running board. They also replaced a half-dozen missing bolts. The rest of the volunteers cleaned—and cleaned. Ten years of neglect had resulted in a mountain of dust, dirt and grime.

"Would it be all right if we gave the wagon a fresh coat of paint?" Caitlin asked. "We'd buy the paint, of course."

"Sure. As long as you use John Deere green."

She laughed. "I think we can manage that. It'll go perfectly with the wreaths and Christmas lights."

The volunteers were taking a well-deserved break, refueling with doughnuts the older gentleman had brought.

"Justin seems taken with Tamiko," Ethan said. He and Caitlin sat on a pair of old crates, away from the rest of the volunteers.

"I noticed that, too." She cast a worried glance at her brother, who maneuvered his wheelchair in order to be closer to the young woman. "I hope she doesn't break his heart."

"Looks to me like she's more interested in him than she is in her boyfriend."

Justin was holding the hose and filling a bucket with water while Tamiko poured in a capful of liquid soap. There was no mistaking the exchange of smiles and frequent eye contact.

"Tamiko's a sweet, funny girl," Caitlin said. "But to be honest, I don't think Justin stands a chance with her."

"Because she already has a boyfriend?"

"That—" Caitlin turned back to Ethan "—and because he's in a wheelchair."

"Don't underestimate him. Or her."

She said nothing, perhaps because this conversation had started to sound too much like the one they'd had in his bunkhouse earlier in the week.

They finished their doughnuts and spent the next several minutes watching an advanced riding class in the arena. Their break would soon be over, and Ethan didn't think he'd have another chance to speak to Caitlin alone.

"About last night..."

She immediately straightened. "We both agreed kissing was a mistake."

"I didn't agree."

"Ethan." She looked over at her crew of volunteers before continuing. "Can we discuss this later?"

"When later?"

"I brought my table and duffel bag. We can have another PT session today if you're available."

"After what you said, I assumed we weren't continuing."

"I told you, a deal's a deal." She gathered up their trash. "Besides, you need physical therapy if that shoulder's going to heal properly."

He did need it, what with the jackpot only a week away.

And the prospect of Caitlin's hands on him, even if they frequently caused him excruciating pain, was too appealing to resist.

CAITLIN WAVED GOODBYE to her brother and friends. Had she been wrong, making arrangements for Justin to return home without her? He sat in the backseat next to Tamiko. Her boyfriend, for some reason, occupied the front passenger seat. Given his angry glare, he wasn't too happy about the arrangement.

Tamiko was only being nice, Caitlin told herself. She wouldn't intentionally lead Justin on. But he was following nonetheless.

Work on the wagon had gone well, better than Caitlin had expected. Her emotional state, however, was in turmoil...a continuation from the previous night and this afternoon.

She should avoid Ethan, her common sense urged. The

problem was they had an agreement, one that would bring them together often in the coming weeks.

The prospect unsettled her. Made her a little nervous.

It also thrilled her.

Telling herself over and over that she was here for one reason only, she returned to her minivan and drove it to the bunkhouse. Ethan wasn't there. He'd left after bidding Caitlin's friends and brother goodbye. She could see him in the round pen across the way, unsaddling Prince under Gavin's watchful eye. Unless she was mistaken, the horse wasn't making much of a fuss.

A step in the right direction.

Hopefully, Prince would be as gentle when the day came for Ethan to ride him.

He'd been lucky last night at the rodeo arena. Very lucky. His next fall could end differently.

She carried her portable table from the van to the bunkhouse, determined to complete the task before Ethan showed up and did it for her. Again. When he arrived a few minutes later, Caitlin, the table and her duffel bag were all waiting on the porch.

"Sorry I'm late," he said, nudging the door open with his good shoulder.

He kept his left arm tucked close to his chest, as he had all morning. What was wrong with her? She should have insisted he leave all the wagon repairs to her crew. But then she wouldn't have enjoyed his company for over two hours.

It reminded her a little of their senior year in high school, when she'd coerced him into helping her with decorations for the winter formal. He'd hated it, and his football teammates had ridiculed him. Still, he'd done everything she'd asked, and though she hadn't appreciated him as much as she should have, she'd never forgotten.

"Have you been icing your shoulder twice a day and taking ibuprofen?"

"Yes, Nurse Carmichael," he teased.

"How much did it hurt last night?"

"Before or after my ride?"

"Both."

"It hurt before. A lot more after."

"Didn't appear to affect your ride much. You lasted eight seconds."

"The horse was having a slow night." Ethan unbuttoned his long-sleeved work shirt, wincing slightly as he peeled it off. "I won't be nearly so fortunate next time."

After only one PT session, he pretty much knew the drill and completed the exercises with minimal instruction from her. She was glad to see he'd found the old set of weights and was using them. His range of motion, she observed, had improved minimally.

When he finished with the exercises, she patted the table. "Ready?"

He hopped on, then lay on his back. "You going to your parents' house for Thanksgiving?" he asked once she began rotating his arm.

She remembered from their first session that Ethan liked to talk during therapy. Justin did, too. It probably helped them tolerate the pain better. Except she wasn't fooled. The strain in their voices along with clenched jaws and muscle tremors gave them away.

"Actually, they're going to my aunt and uncle's in Green Valley."

"Don't your relatives usually come up here?"

"Not this year. Uncle Lee just had back surgery and can't handle a long drive. They invited me and Justin. He hasn't decided for sure, but I'm not going."

"Why not?"

"I'm scheduled to work at the clinic Wednesday evening and will be here Friday morning to work on the wagon. Driving to Green Valley and back in one day is too much for me. I'll be wiped out."

"If you want," Ethan said through gritted teeth as she applied more pressure, "come to the house for dinner."

"I couldn't impose."

"Trust me, you won't be. Dad and Sage are doing all the cooking. Can't guarantee you won't get stuck with cleanup duty."

How many times had she done exactly that after dinner with the Powells? Too many to count. "I don't know...."

"This will be our first Thanksgiving dinner in nine years."

She didn't think he was trying to make her feel guilty as much as expressing his pleasure that the family had finally moved on enough after his mother's death to celebrate the holidays.

"Thank you." She lifted his arm high over his head. "But I'd better not."

"Is it because I kissed you last night?"

"Yes." That was only partially true. The bigger reason was that she'd kissed him back. Enthusiastically. "It wouldn't be right encouraging you when there's no hope of us ever... picking up where we left off." She couldn't bring herself to say *falling in love again.*

"My bronc riding," he said flatly.

"I explained already. And now that you've qualified for the jackpot, I'm assuming there's no chance you'll give it up."

"None."

"Turn on your right side," she instructed, hoping the change in position would put an end to their conversation.

It didn't.

"I care about you, Caitlin. And I think you still care about me."

"Of course I do. Just not like I used to."

"Then why are you always putting up your guard whenever we're together?"

"I'm a nurse." Lifting his shoulder off the table with one hand, she pushed down on his elbow with the other. "You're my patient."

"It's also easier to deny your feelings when you distance yourself."

"You're wrong."

"I don't think so."

The wound she'd believed long healed suddenly tore open, catching her unawares and leaving her feeling vulnerable. "I was devastated when you left."

That got a reaction from him—he winced.

Then again, her fingers were digging with excessive force into the soft tissue surrounding his shoulder.

"I don't regret enlisting, only how I handled telling you." His voice seemed to hold genuine regret.

"What about losing your leg?"

"Don't get me wrong, I'd rather that hadn't happened. But I was luckier than a lot of soldiers. At least I came home."

"I'd have gone with you."

"It doesn't work that way."

"Even if we were married?"

"I wanted to ask you."

"Then why didn't you?" Emotion thickened her voice.

"I was afraid something would happen to me. That I'd be killed and you'd be all alone. Like my father was after my mother died."

"Isn't that what you did? Left me alone? Only, instead of dying, you took off."

Neither of them spoke for a moment, and Caitlin relaxed her grip, the tension seeping out of both of them as she massaged his shoulder, upper arm and back.

Lying on his side, his eyes closed, the dim light softening his features, he looked seventeen again. Caitlin's anger faded, and she felt vulnerable all over, but for different reasons.

"I was an idiot," he said, breaking the silence. "I ran away from the very person I needed the most, because I couldn't handle my grief. You have no idea how much I wish I hadn't."

"Thank you for being honest. But it changes nothing." She stepped away from the table.

He sat up so abruptly the table shook. "That's what you're doing, too, Caitlin. You're running away."

"I wouldn't be here right now if that was true."

"Then come to Thanksgiving dinner."

"I told you, I can't."

"Trust me, I have no expectations where we're concerned—despite the kiss last night." He held up his hand when she would have protested. "We were swept up in the moment is all. No big deal."

Maybe not for him. It had been a very big deal for her.

"Come on." He grinned imploringly. "No one should be alone on Thanksgiving. And Dad would love to see you again."

"Justin may be—"

"Bring him, too. He's more than welcome."

Caitlin couldn't imagine making a bigger mistake, considering her knee-buckling reaction to Ethan's kiss. If only she didn't dread spending Thanksgiving alone in her little condo. And Justin would probably love coming to the ranch....

"All right," she said, relenting. "I accept your invitation. As long as we're clear—*friends only.*"

"Yes, ma'am," he answered, his solemn tone in direct contrast to the twinkle lighting his eyes.

Caitlin sighed tiredly.

Had he heard even one thing she said?

Chapter Seven

Ethan's father stood in front of the open oven door, fussing over the roasting turkey as if he was competing in a professional cook-off and about to be judged.

"It's not browning right."

"Looks okay to me." Ethan peered around his dad's head. "I'm sure it'll taste fine."

"Humph."

Evidently not the right thing to say to someone who took food preparation seriously.

Wayne Powell shut the oven door with more force than was necessary. Grumbling to himself, he went to the counter and checked on the girls. They'd been assigned the task of peeling potatoes, an entire five-pound sack.

He wasn't annoyed with Ethan, at least not as much as he pretended. He liked being in charge of the kitchen, liked making a fuss. Up until Sage and Isa had entered their lives, cooking was the only chore he regularly performed on the ranch, choosing instead to remain a semirecluse. Even Cassie, his one and only grandchild, coming to live with them hadn't rescued him from the deep depression he'd succumbed to after his wife died. All that had changed when the girls went missing.

Finding them in the box canyon had not only resulted in

Prince's capture, it restored Wayne Powell to his former self and his family.

This was truly a day to be thankful.

The reason foremost in Ethan's mind was Caitlin coming to dinner. He hadn't spoken to her about Thanksgiving since inviting her last Saturday, though he'd seen her twice for physical-therapy sessions. He worried that bringing up the topic of dinner might cause her to change her mind. Better to keep cool. Lie low. Feign disinterest.

Yeah, tell that to his gut, which had been churning all morning from nervous tension.

"How's the pico de gallo coming?" Ethan's father asked.

Sage stood at the counter beside the girls, chopping tomatoes, cilantro, green chillies, garlic and onions. "Almost done, and then I'll be out of your way."

Normally Ethan's father would have resisted serving pico de gallo and tortilla chips as an appetizer at Thanksgiving. But he loved Sage and Isa and welcomed their contribution, even if it wasn't a traditional dish.

"Nice day." Gavin appeared at Ethan's side and gave his brother a hand with putting the extra leaf in the dining table. "We haven't had this much commotion in a long time."

"Yeah, real nice." They'd always been a close family. It was just that for the last decade, they'd been a broken one. Like his brother, Ethan was glad to see their family on the mend.

"Too bad Sierra isn't here." Gavin slipped the extra leaf into place, then helped Ethan push the expanded table together.

"I don't know what's wrong with her. She hasn't called yet, and Dad's starting to worry."

"It's still early, and that job of hers keeps her busy."

"On Thanksgiving?"

"It's possible."

Ethan had his doubts. Something was wrong with his sister and had been since her last visit a year and a half ago. Everything had gone well, as far as he knew. Really well. But shortly after she returned to San Francisco, she'd stopped answering her phone, stopped emailing regularly and was always busy when someone did finally get ahold of her.

"Let's wait till dinner's over," Gavin said. "Then we'll call her."

He was always the more reasonable of the two brothers, and Ethan would be wise to listen. Still, he couldn't ignore his instincts, and they warned him to be on the watch where Sierra was concerned.

"I'm going to bring in more wood for the fireplace," he said.

"What about your shoulder?"

"I'm fine." Ethan wasn't exactly fine, though he was considerably improved, thanks to a constant regime of ibuprofen, ice packs and physical therapy. In fact, he was enough better that his confidence was growing. Despite not making eight seconds again since his ride last week, he'd changed his goal from just competing in Saturday's jackpot to placing in the top five positions.

If you want to be a winner, you have to think like one.

His high school coach's advice still rang in Ethan's ears, and he heeded it.

Escaping the bustle of the busy kitchen, he went outside to the woodpile behind the house. On his third trip carrying an armful of cut pine logs, he spied Clay's truck pulling through the main gate. His renewed friendship with his childhood buddy was yet another reason to be thankful today.

"Need a hand?" Clay asked, meeting him on the back porch.

"I think I've got enough for now." Ethan did let Clay open the door for him. "See your dad today?"

"Nope."

"Talk to him?"

No answer.

"Isn't it about time you two buried the hatchet?"

"We will. One day. Just not yet."

Clay and his father had suffered a terrible falling-out when Bud Duvall had refused to honor his agreement with Ethan's dad and had sold the Powell land out from under them. There was likely more to the story, but Clay chose not to elaborate, and Ethan respected his friend's privacy.

Taking his share of money from the family's cattle operation, Clay had struck out on his own, purchasing a large parcel of land a few miles down the road. He'd used the remaining funds to construct the rodeo arena and bankroll his rodeo stock business. Somewhere in between, he'd married and, after six short months, divorced. But that subject was also off-limits.

While Clay shook hands and dispensed hugs to the other Powell family members, Ethan carried the last load of firewood into the living room, placing it in the log bin along with the rest. He was just glancing at the mantel clock and wondering if Caitlin had changed her mind, after all, when a small commotion rose from the kitchen.

"Nurse Carmichael's here!" Cassie's high-pitched voice echoed throughout the house.

Ethan headed for the kitchen, presenting a welcoming smile that he hoped hid the turmoil in his heart. Caitlin wanted to be friends, and he'd rather have her in his life as a friend than not at all.

It wasn't, however, what *he* wanted.

"Happy Thanksgiving."

He envied the girls, who clung to her with the tenacity of baby possums riding their mother's back.

"Same to you." She smiled brightly. "Sorry we're late."

To his delight, she extracted herself from the girls' clutches and gave him a casual but decidedly warm hug. He resisted the urge to fold her in his arms and bury his face in the soft, fragrant skin of her neck.

Justin appeared in the doorway, having taken a bit longer to cross the porch. He rolled his wheelchair over the threshold and into the kitchen, which was now crowded with nine people.

"Hi, everybody."

Reintroductions were made along with new ones. When it came to Isa, the little girl hovered behind her mother. She wasn't normally shy, and Ethan suspected Justin's wheelchair had something to do with the change in her behavior.

"Hello, I'm Justin." He tilted his head so he could see her better and winked. "What's your name?"

"Isa," she answered timidly.

"Well, Isa, I was hoping for a tour of the house. Maybe you can show me around."

She crouched even farther behind Sage.

"That's too bad. Because I brought this box of chocolates, and I need someone to help me eat them." He produced a wrapped package from the backpack on his lap. "Possibly two someones."

That was enough encouragement for Cassie. She rushed forward. "Can I touch your chair?"

"Sure." Justin shifted sideways, and Cassie stroked the armrest.

"Wow!" She bent and examined the wheels. "Cool."

Isa slowly emerged from behind her mother to stand next to Cassie. At Justin's smile of encouragement, she also stroked the wheelchair's armrest.

"Come on, you two. Let's get out of here before the grown-ups put us to work."

"Yeah," Cassie agreed. "I hate peeling potatoes."

Including himself with the "kids," even though he was considerably older than them, sealed the deal. Justin and his young tour guides left the kitchen to explore the rest of the house.

Caitlin's smile followed them.

"He's very good with children," Sage observed.

"He's going be a teacher when he graduates."

"A good one, it looks like."

"What can I do to help?" Caitlin held up a container. "I brought a pumpkin pie."

She was instantly recruited to slice the freshly baked bread.

Ethan offered Clay a beer. Gavin joined them, and the three men retreated to the calm of the living room. Taking a seat on the couch, Ethan stared at the fire with its leaping flames and crackling logs. The woodsy scent filled the room, giving it that special holiday feeling.

"Sounds like the girls have coaxed Justin into a game of Uno," Gavin said, craning his neck to see through the archway and into the family room.

"He's a good sport," Ethan answered.

"A real nice guy," Clay concurred, and took a long swallow of his beer. "Shame about the accident."

"Doesn't seem to have slowed him down any."

"You're right about that." He turned to Ethan. "How's the physical therapy going with Caitlin?"

"Great. I have an appointment at the clinic tomorrow. I'm sure the doctor won't find anything."

"I wasn't talking about your shoulder." Clay shot Gavin a conspiratorial look.

Ethan's brother shrugged.

"Caitlin and I are friends," Ethan insisted. "That's all."

Maybe if he said it seven hundred more times, he'd start believing it.

"You weren't acting like friends the other night when you were kissing." Clay looked at Gavin again and received another shrug.

Ethan sipped his beer. He and Caitlin hadn't acted like friends when they were kissing because it hadn't felt that way.

"What are you going to do?" Clay asked.

"Nothing. She says there's no chance for us as long as I'm riding broncs and breaking horses."

"Then give it up."

"Are you nuts?"

"Isn't she worth it?"

Conner had made a similar comment the other night at the rodeo arena.

"It's not like I wouldn't—won't—give up bronc riding eventually." When he'd erased all doubt from his and everyone else's minds that he was no different than before the car bomb explosion. "Breaking horses, that's another thing. It's my job."

"She's the love of your life."

"*Former* love of my life," he corrected. "And that was years ago."

"She could be again." Clay sent Gavin another look. This one was met with a confident nod.

Ethan was less sure about his feelings for Caitlin and hers for him. Could he ever give up his cowboy ways for her? He'd almost rather lose his other leg.

It was a quandary he continued to ponder all through dinner as he sat across the large table from her. He did his best to keep up with the lively conversations, but was completely distracted by her green eyes and the memory of them drifting shut as his mouth claimed hers.

"I HAD A WONDERFUL TIME. Thank you so much for inviting us." Caitlin wrapped her arms around Wayne Powell's generous waist and squeezed.

He returned the hug with great enthusiasm. "It's wonderful to have you back. Just like old times."

She agreed. The only difference was the absence of his late wife, who'd been mentioned often during dinner.

"Give your parents my regards." Wayne released Caitlin. "And don't be a stranger, you hear?" He tapped the tip of her nose with his finger.

"I won't."

If only Caitlin was certain she could return for a social visit. No matter how often she told herself she wasn't interested in Ethan romantically, there was no denying the rush of awareness that stole over her whenever she caught his dark eyes observing her.

"Goodbye, Justin." Isa hung on to his wheelchair, which earlier in the day had intimidated her. "If you come back, I'll let you ride my horse, Chico."

"Deal, kiddo." He bumped fists with her before wheeling himself through the back door.

Caitlin's steps momentarily faltered. Was Isa's invitation spur-of-the-moment or had Justin and the girls been talking about riding? Considering his last visit to the ranch, Caitlin should have seen this coming.

"I'm right behind you," she called to her brother, who beat her out the door.

She'd said her farewells to everyone except Ethan, who'd disappeared at the last second. She tried not to let the obvious slight bother her. They'd see each other again tomorrow when she and her volunteers came by to work on the wagon.

Sound reasoning did nothing to alleviate her disappointment.

"Take your time," Justin called to her.

She scarcely noticed the hint of amusement in his tone, she was so distracted. Once outside, she almost ran over Ethan.

"I'll walk you to your car."

That would probably be a mistake. It would be much less nerve-racking to say goodbye here, with his family watching from the doorway. Only she didn't, and he fell into step beside her.

Lately, it seemed, the harder she tried to keep him at a distance, the closer he got.

Or was it the closer she allowed him to get?

"Thanks again for coming," he said.

She hoped he wouldn't take her hand, as he had in the bunkhouse. Touching him would break down the last of her defenses.

"I really enjoyed myself. Justin did, too."

"Dad insists I ask you back."

"That was nice of him."

No commitments. Better for both of them in the long run.

"What time will you be here tomorrow? I'll make sure everything's ready."

"Really," she insisted, "I don't want to put you through any more trouble than I already have. It's enough that you're letting us use your wagon during the festival—and will be driving it."

"I like your friends. And I like you."

Here was where she was supposed to say, "I like you, too," but that would be asking for trouble.

"Let's schedule one last physical-therapy session before the jackpot," she said instead. "How about tomorrow after we're done working on the wagon?"

"Yeah, sure. I appreciate all you've done. My shoulder's doing great."

Justin had already hoisted himself into the front passenger seat and collapsed his wheelchair, leaning it against the open door. Ethan went over to him, and, after saying goodbye, grabbed the chair.

Caitlin knew better than to insist he let her get it. When-ever Ethan was around, he carried things. Maybe to show everyone he wasn't an invalid. More likely, that was the way Wayne Powell had raised his sons.

When Ethan had finished loading the chair, he came around to join her at the driver's-side door. For an awkward second or two, Caitlin debated what to do.

"See you tomorrow," he said.

"Ten sharp."

Another second passed. Two. Three.

Oh, what the hell, she thought. Throwing caution to the wind, she looped her arms around his neck for what was sup-posed to be a brief, casual hug....

Only she was the one to hold on, not Ethan.

The day had been filled with memories. Of the ranch house. Thanksgiving dinner. The Powell family. In truth, the past two weeks had been a constant trip down memory lane. She'd responded to Ethan's kiss the other night out of habit, her body instinctively nestling against his as it had so often in the past.

As it did now.

Emotions, tender and bittersweet, weakened her resolve. She leaned into him and rested her head in the crook of his neck. He stroked her hair, then combed his fingers through it. Another familiar gesture that stirred yet more memories.

She removed her arms, now strangely limp, from around his neck. "I have to go."

"Take care."

Thankfully, Ethan didn't acknowledge the hug.

It would serve her right if he did, after she'd been so ada-mant that there could never be anything between them again.

Before she quite knew what was happening, she was standing on her tiptoes and pressing her lips to his cheek, her hands resting gently on his chest.

He smelled amazing. Fresh and clean like the outdoors, where he spent most of his time. His flannel shirt was smooth beneath her palms, and the bristles of his five o'clock shadow tickled her lips. She shivered ever so slightly.

I wish you hadn't left.

The thought came from nowhere. No, not nowhere. It came from a tiny corner of her heart where it had remained lodged for nine long years.

Mystified and annoyed at what had come over her, she backed away from Ethan, ready to apologize for her lack of control.

One look at his nonchalant expression and she promptly shut her mouth.

Seriously! Was she the only one whose world was just rocked?

Evidently so.

Muttering something unintelligible, Caitlin dived into the minivan, dreading having to explain her actions to Justin.

How could she expect Ethan to believe all her talk about them being just friends when she'd rushed headlong over the line she'd vehemently insisted he not cross?

Chapter Eight

Caitlin stood over a box of Christmas decorations, painstakingly unraveling a knotted mess that promised to be a string of lights. Over in the round pen, Ethan was working with Prince. He hadn't stopped by to help her and her crew, hadn't even waved at them. Considering the way they'd parted yesterday, he was undoubtedly avoiding her. With good reason. One minute she was insisting they couldn't see each other, and the next she was, well, all over him.

The sound of happy laughter distracted her, and she looked over at her brother and Tamiko. They were attempting to twine a string of lights through the spokes of a wagon wheel, and it didn't seem to matter that their efforts weren't producing the desired results. They were having fun.

There was a lesson in there somewhere for Caitlin. She worked too hard. Not just at her various jobs, but at making her and Justin's lives safe. Predictable. Structured. Comfortable.

Thinking back, she hadn't been playing it safe when she'd responded to Ethan's potent kiss at the rodeo arena, or when she'd lost her head yesterday during their hug.

Her glance fell again on Justin and Tamiko. Too bad Tamiko already had a boyfriend. She and Justin were cute together. As she bent close to talk to him, her long black hair fell like a silky curtain, momentarily shielding them from view.

Attraction at its earliest and most innocent.

Perhaps not so innocent, given the yearning in her brother's eyes when Tamiko straightened.

Caitlin's heart broke a little. Her brother was obviously smitten and understandably so. Tamiko was gorgeous, bright and chock-full of personality. But she was also taken. Compared to the strong and towering young man painting the wagon's sidewall, Caitlin doubted her brother stood a snowball's chance. Tamiko was simply being kind to him, not realizing how hard and fast he was falling for her.

Caitlin chuckled mirthlessly to herself. She and her brother were quite the pair. Here he was chasing a girl who wasn't available, while she was trying her hardest to stop Ethan from chasing her.

"You finished with that string of lights?" Howard asked.

"Almost." Caitlin smiled. The older man had turned out to be a big help.

She and her crew of volunteers weren't the only people at the ranch this Friday morning after Thanksgiving. At least a dozen riders were exercising their horses in the main arena. Another group was readying for a trail ride. In a small arena adjacent to the main one, a lone woman riding with an English saddle took her horse over a series of jumps. Clay and four or five of his men were hard at it, hammering, sawing and raising a ruckus as they labored to convert the old cattle barn into a mare motel. Once in a while, one or two of the men wandered over to Ethan's bunkhouse, carrying a toolbox or a ladder or sheets of drywall.

Gavin waved to her as he left the barn and headed to the round pen.

Caitlin did a double take. Ethan had finally gotten a saddle and bridle on the mustang. She stopped working on the lights to watch.

The moment Gavin reached the pen, he and Ethan entered into a heated discussion. Ethan waved off his brother, who in turn demanded to be heard. When Ethan didn't respond, Gavin climbed through the rails and into the pen. The argument continued.

Prince behaved relatively well, all things considered. He was calmer, at least, than when Caitlin and Justin had visited him in his stall. Then again, these were the two people who spent the most time with him, and he was used to them.

The brothers' loud voices eventually drew a crowd of ranch hands. Clay emerged from the barn and, after quickly assessing the situation, hurried over.

Gavin cautioned everyone to stay back. He stood at Prince's head, gripping the lead rope attached to the halter Prince wore beneath his bridle. Ethan positioned himself at the horse's right side, the reins bunched in one hand. With his other, he stroked Prince's neck over and over.

Suddenly, he lifted his good leg and placed his foot in the stirrup.

He was going to ride Prince!

Caitlin dropped the lights and ran toward the round pen to join the others.

"Hey, come back," Howard called after her.

She ignored him.

"Sis!"

She slowed for Justin, who quickly caught up with her.

"Where are you going?"

"Ethan's riding Prince."

"Cool."

That wasn't how she would describe it.

She wormed her way between two ranch hands. As much

as watching Ethan terrified her, she had to be there in case something went wrong.

Through the railings, she saw Ethan swing up into the saddle. Prince stood still, a perplexed expression on his face. He slowly craned his head around and sniffed Ethan's leg, his ears twitching. Snorting once, he turned away.

Caitlin expelled a giant sigh of relief. Everything was going to be okay. All that worrying, and Prince was a lamb at heart. Once again she'd overreacted.

"Good boy," Ethan murmured to the horse.

Suddenly, Prince emitted an ear-piercing squeal, his entire body quivering. With no warning whatsoever, he started bucking in place again and again. Ethan was shaken so violently, his hat flew off. Just as quickly, he was flung backward when Prince reared.

By some miracle, he hung on.

The ranch hand beside Caitlin gave a loud whoop and jostled his neighbor's arm. "Did ya see that? Ride 'em, Ethan!"

Caitlin stared, transfixed. She hadn't been this afraid since the day of Justin's accident.

THE TECHNIQUES USED FOR breaking a green horse weren't the same as for riding a bucking bronc.

Ethan transferred all his weight to the lower half of his body. Sitting squarely in the saddle, he pointed his heels toward the ground and squeezed Prince's flanks with his calves. His goal was to hang on until the horse tired, which he hoped would be soon.

He heard his name being called above the whoops and hollers of the people watching him, and thought he caught a glimpse of Caitlin from the corner of his eye. Prince twisted sideways, and from then on, all of Ethan's attention was focused on outlasting the horse on their wild roller-coaster ride. With both hands gripping the reins, he pulled back, keeping

Prince's head tucked close to his body, and preventing him from rearing. Gavin stood in the pen, dashing out of harm's way when necessary, but otherwise keeping a close watch on horse and rider.

Clumps of dirt exploded from beneath Prince's hooves as he bucked and bucked, showering nearby spectators. Ethan barely noticed. This was a contest of wills, and he had every intention of winning.

As suddenly as it started, the rocking motion ceased. Prince transitioned into a choppy lope, lungs heaving and nostrils flaring. Ethan took a chance and gave the horse a little more rein. Prince extended his forelegs, and the ride became considerably smoother.

Cheers and applause erupted. Gavin wore a grin the size of a dinner plate. Ethan's chest swelled with satisfaction and accomplishment. This was hardly the first horse he'd broken, but it was definitely the best.

Prince, always eager to be the center of attention, shifted into a high-stepping trot. Head raised, tail arched, he showed off in front of his admirers, understanding on some level that he was equally interesting to them with a human on his back as he was without one.

Ethan let the horse have his fun. Hell, he was having fun, too. The time of his life. One of his first questions to the doctors when he'd woke after losing his leg was whether he would ever ride again.

They'd uttered all the platitudes, that anything was possible with hard work and determination. But Ethan had glimpsed the uncertainty in their earnest expressions.

Too bad those doctors weren't here now. Not only could he ride, he could break green horses and compete in saddle bronc events. He might even win at the jackpot tomorrow. It was less of a long shot today than it had been yesterday.

After a few more circuits of the pen, Ethan brought Prince

to a halt and dismounted with Gavin's help. He held out the reins to his brother.

"Your turn."

Gavin took them. "Thanks." He clapped Ethan on the shoulder—his *good* shoulder. "For everything."

Ethan heard what his brother didn't say. There had been a time, after the explosion and during rehab, when Ethan wasn't sure if he wanted to come home and help his family with the failing remains of their once thriving cattle operation. Coping with that loss on a daily basis was more than Ethan could handle. But he had come home, and together he, his brother and father built a new business with the potential to be just as profitable as the old one. Adapt or perish. Wasn't that the saying?

The Powells had adapted and, despite the odds, were succeeding.

Ethan held Prince's lead rope while Gavin swung up into the saddle. The horse's eyes went wide at this sudden change, and he initially balked. Once Gavin was situated, however, he settled down, obediently trotting in a circle.

Ethan moved to the center of the pen, watching Prince and making mental notes for future training sessions.

"See if you can get him to lope," he instructed Gavin.

Prince did, after significant urging. Even then, he refused to lead with his left leg. Training him would take patience and a strong hand. Ethan couldn't wait. And once Prince was fully broke, his intelligence and reliable disposition proved, his value as a stud would increase.

Gavin finished his ride. Ethan once again held Prince's head so his brother could dismount without incident. The horse was doing well for a first day, but he was unpredictable at best, and it was wise to err on the side of caution.

If anything, the crowd had grown in size. Caitlin, Ethan noticed, had yet to move from her spot at the fence.

He went first out the gate, keeping the admirers at a safe distance while Gavin led the horse away. Ethan watched them go, his elation giving way to disappointment.

They had agreed that Ethan would break the horse. In some ways, and on most days, he worked more closely with Prince than his brother did. But there was no doubt Gavin and the horse shared a special bond. It had been Gavin who'd tracked the horse for months and insisted on capturing him. Gavin who'd juggled the family's finances so they could purchase Prince at auction, only to lose him to Clay. Gavin who'd set his differences aside in order to form a partnership with Clay that would benefit them both.

Prince knew who was responsible for his cushy new lifestyle. From the moment they'd brought him to the ranch, he'd tolerated Gavin best, allowing him into his stall when no one else could get within ten feet of him. It had been Gavin's jacket pockets he nuzzled, searching for treats.

Ethan wasn't one to waste time envying others, but his brother did have it all. A beautiful, wonderful fiancée who came with a great kid. A terrific daughter. A job he loved. Loyal employees. Friends. Respect in the community. An incredible horse.

Ethan wouldn't mind having a few of those things for himself.

A voice behind him roused him from his reverie.

"Hell of a ride, pal!" A beaming Clay handed Ethan his hat.

"We still have a long way to—"

"I swear," one of the wranglers interrupted Ethan, "I've never seen anything like that."

Someone else shook his hand. Then another person. His father was there, too. Ethan didn't remember seeing him at the round pen. The next thing he knew, he was pulled into a mighty bear hug.

"I'm proud of you, son."

Ethan swallowed, his throat tightening. "Thanks, Dad."

He recalled a similar celebration when he'd just returned home from rehab. His father had expressed his pride then, too. But there had been an underlying sadness to the gathering of friends and family that dampened the mood.

Ethan had been a wounded man.

Now he was a warrior once again.

And the person he wanted most to share this incredible moment with was Caitlin.

Where had she gone?

He searched for her, spotting her with Justin on the fringes of the now dispersing crowd. He made his way over to her, mindless of the people calling his name and tugging on his jacket sleeves.

Justin's boyish face lit with pleasure at the sight of Ethan. "Dude, that was awesome! I took pictures with my phone. Here, I'll show you." He started fiddling with the device. "Darn it," he grumbled when the photos didn't immediately fill the screen. "Hold on a second."

Ethan gave Caitlin a crooked smile. "Did you see?"

"Yes."

He'd been so caught up with his ride and how great it had gone, he hadn't really looked at her. She wasn't smiling, and her brows were drawn together in a pronounced V.

"Is something wrong?" he asked.

"Not at all."

"She was worried you were going to fall," Justin answered.

"But I didn't fall."

"You could have." Again Justin replied for his sister.

She glared at him.

"Hey, don't get mad at me. It's true."

"I break three or four horses a month," Ethan said. "If not

one of Clay's rodeo stock, then a client's horse. I'm good at my job."

"She gets scared easily."

"All right!" Caitlin snapped. "I do get scared easily. Who wouldn't? The horse was going crazy."

Ethan liked that she worried about him. It was another sign she cared. What he didn't like was her disapproval, which was tarnishing an otherwise memorable day for him and his family.

"You're upset with me," she said.

"Of course not." Only he was.

"Here we go," Justin announced enthusiastically, and passed Ethan his phone.

There were five photos, two fuzzy and out of focus. In one, Ethan's head and Prince's legs were cut off. The remaining two were quite good for having been taken with a cell phone.

He tried to see his ride through Caitlin's eyes. Prince, his nose to the ground, his back legs straight up in the air, could appear dangerous to a novice. But not once had Ethan lost control or so much as slipped in the saddle. Surely she'd seen that. Everyone else had, and was thrilled and excited for him.

"Thanks, bud." He returned the phone to Justin.

"I can email these to you if you want."

"That'd be great. I'll have Gavin post them on the ranch's website."

"Hey, Caitlin!" Howard hollered though cupped hands. "We have a problem."

"I need to go." She started out at a brisk walk.

"Wait!" Ethan went after her, cursing himself.

She stopped and pivoted slowly.

"Why can't you be happy for me?" he asked.

"I am."

"You have a strange way of showing it. I rode Prince. I'm fine. Not a single scratch."

"You're right."

"I get that you're scared."

"I don't think you do." Her voice shook. "I don't think you have the slightest inkling of how truly terrified I was, watching you ride."

"Caitlin—"

"I admit it, I'm a neurotic mess."

"You're not neurotic. A little obsessive, maybe."

"This isn't a matter of whether my worrying is obsessive or reasonable." She placed a hand over her heart. "It's how I feel, and it won't change or go away because you or I want it to."

"I'm sorry."

"Me, too." She walked away from him then.

Ethan stared after her. Until that instant, he hadn't believed their differences were insurmountable.

No more.

"GO EASY ON HER."

It took Ethan a few seconds to realize Justin had wheeled up beside him. "Yeah?"

"She's crazy about you."

It went both ways. "Could've fooled me."

Ethan wasn't sure where he should go—after Caitlin, back to the stables or to the office. "You want a beer?"

Justin glanced at his watch, shrugged, then grinned. "Sure. I'm not driving. Nothing motorized, anyway."

"Let's go."

Neither said a word on the short walk to Ethan's bunkhouse until they reached the porch.

"Can you—"

"No problem."

Justin reversed his wheelchair and backed it up to the bottom step. Leaning forward, he cranked the wheels and climbed the two short steps inch by grueling inch, the muscles in his arms straining.

"You're pretty good at that."

"I've had a lot of practice." Justin maneuvered the chair through the bunkhouse door, which was just wide enough to accommodate him. "This is nice," he said, and parked himself adjacent to the couch.

Why his sister constantly fretted about him, Ethan didn't understand. Justin was obviously capable of handling himself.

Ethan recalled his own months of rehab, learning how to stand, walk off a curb, climb a ladder, manage stairs. More than once he'd landed face-first on the floor.

"Thanks," Justin said, when he passed him a cold beer from the refrigerator.

Ethan sank onto the couch and propped his feet on the old footlocker that served as a coffee table. The beer tasted good, and for several moments they savored it in silence.

"It's not Caitlin's fault she's the way she is," Justin said finally.

"It's not your fault, either."

"Hell, no, it's not." He took a swig of beer. "She changed after the accident. We all did."

"I can relate." Ethan lifted his bottle in a toast, which Justin returned.

"Don't take this wrong, okay? But when you lost your leg, your family wasn't there. They didn't see you at the hospital afterward."

That was true. Gavin had wanted to fly out to Germany, where Ethan had been transferred for surgery immediately after being stabilized. Unfortunately, the ranch was barely sustaining itself in those days, and they didn't have the money to finance a trip to Tucson, much less halfway around the world.

"Caitlin and my parents spent some pretty harrowing weeks while I was in a medically induced coma. They didn't know if I'd survive, much less walk again."

"I can imagine."

"Caitlin blamed herself, which was ridiculous. I chose to jump off that cliff. She had nothing to do with it. I was bound and determined to show everyone I wasn't the loser they called me behind my back and to my face."

Justin's need to prove himself in front of others was a lot like Ethan's—except his attempt had ended in tragedy. Ethan had a decidedly different outcome in mind for himself.

"Have you told her you don't hold her responsible?"

"Dude, I've practically had it engraved in stone. She doesn't listen."

Ethan pondered Justin's remark while finishing the last of his beer. "Want another one?"

"Sure. Why not? I doubt Caitlin's missing me."

"Caitlin or that girl? What's her name?"

"Tamiko."

"She's cute."

"And has a boyfriend."

"You haven't let anything stop you from doing what you want before now." Ethan retrieved two fresh beers from the refrigerator.

"Her boyfriend, Eric, may be dumber than a bag of hammers, but I think he can take me."

"It's not his decision who she dates. It's hers."

"You're right." Justin copied Ethan and raised his beer in a toast. "And the same could be said for you, my friend."

"About Caitlin?"

"You want her. Don't let anything stop you."

"I'm up against a lot more than a boyfriend. You saw her

today. A five-ton steamroller couldn't break through those walls she's erected."

"Chicken."

"Me?" Ethan snorted. "Have you looked in the mirror lately?"

Justin laughed. "Tell you what, let's make a deal. I'll go after Tamiko and you go after my sister. Who knows? Maybe we'll both get lucky."

Ethan stood and hitched up his jeans. "You're on."

Justin's challenge might have been issued in jest, but Ethan took it seriously. If any two people deserved a second chance, he and Caitlin did—and he was determined to see they got it.

Chapter Nine

"Is it gonna hurt?" The little girl's eyes brimmed with unshed tears.

"No, I promise, sweetie." Caitlin dabbed antibiotic ointment onto the girl's cut with a cotton swab. "There, see?"

"Ow!" She jerked her knee away, although the ointment couldn't possibly have stung.

The cut wasn't serious. Caitlin had seen far worse this past week alone.

"I don't know how she fell." The mother anxiously smoothed her daughter's disheveled hair. "I swear she wasn't out of my sight more than a minute."

"We were running, and Becky Lynn pushed me."

The girl sat in a folding chair, the same one Ethan had occupied when Caitlin had examined his shoulder, and again when she'd helped him put his prosthesis back on. She hoped to see him today—safe and sound after his ride, not in the first-aid station for a third time.

"You and Becky Lynn have to be careful." The mother hovered, watching every move as Caitlin placed a bandage over the cut and pressed down on the adhesive tabs. "There are a lot of people here today. You shouldn't be running around and not paying attention."

There *were* a lot of people. Caitlin hadn't known how many to expect, considering this was Clay's first jackpot.

Someone mentioned fifty-six entrants had registered and by Caitlin's estimation at least two hundred people packed the bleachers.

The little girl was Caitlin's second patient this afternoon, and the event hadn't officially started yet. She'd also treated one of Clay's wranglers after a bull stomped on his foot while they were transferring livestock from the paddocks to the holding pens behind the chutes. Though the cowboy's foot was only bruised and not broken, she'd advised him to take it easy for the rest of the day.

FYI, he hadn't. She'd seen him twice so far, limping as he went about his tasks.

He reminded her of Ethan.

"Can I go now?"

"Sure thing." Caitlin rolled down the little girl's pant leg, covering the bandage.

She hopped off the chair and flexed her knee as if testing the bandage's sticking power.

"What do I owe you?" her mother asked.

"Not a thing. It's part of the service."

"You sure? I really appreciate the help."

"If you'd like, you can make a donation to the Powells' Wild Mustang Sanctuary. There's a collection jar at the chuck wagon."

"I will." The woman's tentative smile bloomed.

Her daughter tugged on her hand. "Hurry, Mommy. We don't want to miss Daddy's ride."

"Oh, honey, don't worry. The bull riders go last, after the bronc riders."

Caitlin thought of Ethan breaking Prince yesterday.

"Isn't it hard watching your husband ride bulls?" she asked the woman, surprised at the boldness of her question. "Aren't you afraid for him?"

"'Course I'm afraid. I start shaking the second that chute

opens, and don't stop till he waves at me from the other side of the arena fence."

"Why put yourself through that?"

Why let him do it? was what she really wanted to know.

"My Micky's no champion bull rider and not likely to ever be one. These jackpots, they're his moment to shine, you know? For eight seconds, he's king of the world. I wouldn't dare miss it, and I wouldn't dare take it away from him, either."

"Mommy!" The little girl tugged harder on her hand. "Let's go."

"You be careful," Caitlin told the girl. "I don't want to see you back here."

"And I'll be sure to put a donation in that collection jar," the mother promised as they left.

Caitlin spent the next several minutes cleaning up after her patient and thinking about the woman's remarks. Her support of her husband was admirable. But what if he fell and hurt himself? His loving wife and beautiful daughter depended on him. He put not only himself at risk when he went into the arena, but his family, too.

"Hey." Clay's large frame filled the doorway. "I see you've had a couple visitors already today."

"Your wrangler T.J. was one of them. He should be resting somewhere, elevating and icing that foot," she admonished.

"I told him to take the day off."

"FYI, he didn't listen to you."

"He needs the money, Caitlin. It's a tough economy, and he has bills to pay."

"Right."

"You annoyed at me specifically or the world in general?"

"Sorry." Caitlin was immediately contrite. "That was uncalled for."

"Does your mood have anything to do with Ethan competing?"

"Not at all."

"You sure?" Clay stepped fully into the room. "Because he mentioned you being mad at him. Something to do with breaking Prince yesterday."

Caitlin hadn't been particularly close to Clay when they were younger, even though he was Ethan's best friend. They were always in competition for Ethan's time and attention. Caitlin had wanted him to herself, while Clay was constantly luring Ethan away for football or rodeo or fishing or a night out with the boys.

Working for Clay, however, had changed their relationship. He really was a decent guy, and Caitlin felt bad that his brief marriage had ended disastrously.

"A couple of weeks ago he injured his shoulder," she told Clay. "Then his prosthesis came off. Next time could be a lot worse."

"He knows what he's doing."

"He's at a disadvantage. I heard him telling Justin at Thanksgiving dinner he sometimes has trouble keeping weight on his left leg, and it throws him off balance."

"He's learned to compensate."

"How would you feel if something happened to him?"

"Like shit," Clay answered honestly. "But I wouldn't blame myself, if that's what you're asking."

"Not even a little? You did give him permission to enter the jackpot."

"He's a grown man. He makes his own decisions."

Ethan had tried to tell her the same thing about Justin. That he was the one who chose to jump off the cliff.

But there was a difference. While Clay allowed Ethan to ride broncs and enter the jackpot, he hadn't encouraged him. Goaded him. If anything, he'd discouraged Ethan.

"You care, and that's sweet." Clay watched her as she meticulously organized the tray of supplies. "Did you ever think your constant worrying makes him feel like an invalid and not like the normal guy he wants to be?"

Her hand slipped, knocking a box of gauze pads to the floor. She stooped to pick it up. "Did he tell you that?"

"Not in so many words."

"I don't think of him as an invalid."

"You just said he's at a disadvantage because of his artificial leg. That sounds like you're calling him an invalid."

"I'm not," she argued hotly. "Not on purpose."

"Then go watch him compete. Saddle bronc riding is the first event."

"Leave the first-aid station? What if someone gets injured?"

"This place isn't that big." Clay grinned affably. "We'll find you."

"I…can't."

"Why not?"

"Watching him would be like giving my stamp of approval, and I don't approve. It has nothing to do with his prosthesis. Anyone who climbs on a bull or bronc is an idiot in my opinion."

Clay's response was a loud laugh.

"This isn't funny."

"You're right." He promptly sobered, studying her intently. "What?"

"I was just thinking how lucky Ethan is to have you."

"He doesn't *have* me."

Clay laughed again. Her steely glare had no effect on silencing him.

The overhead speakers did the trick when they came to life and a man's crackling voice announced the start of the jackpot.

"I'd better get going." Clay hesitated at the door. "Hope you change your mind about watching Ethan."

"I won't."

"This is a big moment for him. He wants you there."

Caitlin was still thinking about what Clay had said five minutes later as she listened to the announcer call the names of the first three contestants.

How many men were competing in bronc riding today and how soon until Ethan's turn?

What did it matter? She wasn't going to watch him. She managed to stick to her guns until the announcer, during color commentary between participants, mentioned the Powells, their mustang sanctuary and Ethan's military service.

Caitlin dashed out the door and raced toward the area behind the bucking chutes where the cowboys typically gathered to debate the various merits of the bucking stock. He was there, engrossed in conversation with two men.

He noticed her only when one of his companions elbowed him in the ribs and nodded in her direction. If he was surprised to see her, he hid it well.

She slowed, her courage evaporating as quickly as it had come.

He broke away from his friends and met her halfway, ignoring the good-humored jeers they hurled after him.

"Hey."

"I…uh…" She tipped her head back in order to see his face, and promptly lost her train of thought. His dark eyes had a way of doing that to her.

"If you're here to tell me I shouldn't ride, you've wasted a trip."

"I'm not."

His brows rose. "Good."

"I didn't want you getting on that horse thinking I was mad at you. I'm not, and I apologize for my behavior yesterday. I really am happy you broke Prince and proud that you're competing today."

"Thanks." His mouth lifted in a sexy, knee-weakening grin. "Don't suppose I could have a kiss. For luck."

She should have seen that coming. "How 'bout a hug?"

"I'll take what I can get."

Determined not to lose control as she had during their last hug, she looped her arms around his neck, her spine ramrod straight, her cheek averted. She lasted two full seconds before her entire body melted with a gentle sigh and she relaxed into his embrace.

When they parted, he caught her chin between his thumb and forefinger. "I'm going the full eight seconds."

"I just want you to be safe." Her voice quavered.

"I can do both."

She carried that promise with her to the stands, where she perched on the front row of the bleachers, her foot tapping nervously.

ETHAN WATCHED CAITLIN walk away, her hands stuffed in the pockets of her hoodie, her slim shoulders hunched. It wasn't cold. In fact, the sun shone brightly in a perfect, cloudless sky. But Caitlin looked cold.

Or was she sad?

"Hey, Powell!"

Hearing his name, he sauntered back to his buddies. He couldn't afford to be distracted, by Caitlin or anyone. His upcoming ride was too important. He'd made it this far, paying the price in pain and sweat, and refused to screw up.

"You drew a mean one."

Micky's comment prompted Ethan to reevaluate Batteries Included, the bronc he was about to take for a spin. He'd helped train the big, rangy black, one of Clay's first purchases when he'd started his rodeo stock business, and knew to expect the unexpected. Batteries Included possessed enough bucking power to give a cowboy a championship ride, if he could stay in the saddle. Most who rode the horse ended up in a pile on the arena floor.

Ethan didn't plan on joining their ranks.

"You ready?" Micky asked.

There was a lot that could be read into the question. Was he ready to make a fool of himself in front of a huge crowd? Or was he ready to show everyone he still had what it took to compete professionally, even if he couldn't enter Professional Rodeo Cowboys Association—sanctioned rodeos?

Micky could also be wondering something as simple as whether or not Ethan had his nerves under control.

The answer to that last question was no. He hadn't been this jittery since he was fourteen and competing in his first junior rodeo. He'd fared poorly, getting bucked off in every event. He'd also learned many valuable lessons that stayed with him even today.

"I'm ready," he said, nodding confidently. "Ready to beat the two of you and look damn good doing it."

The three men chuckled.

Letting loose took a little of the edge off his tension and, oddly enough, helped him concentrate.

They moved from the stock pens to the chutes, where they discussed in detail the competitors going before them. Micky straddled the top railing, worming his way between a pair of cousins from Tucson, while Ethan stood beside T.J., his left leg braced on the bottom railing. He could climb the fence, and would have, were he not competing shortly. No point putting unnecessary strain on his prosthesis.

A dozen men were ahead of him, allowing him time to wait. To think. To stress. To envision the worst…and the best.

All day long he'd glimpsed people staring at him, wearing

he-must-be-crazy expressions. Who entered rodeo jackpots with a missing leg?

Half a leg, Ethan corrected.

What was the difference? Half or whole, he was still handicapped.

God, he hated that word, and refused to let it define him.

He searched the audience until he found his family. Gavin, their dad, his niece Cassie, Sage and her daughter, Isa. He didn't want to disappoint them. His brother and father especially. He owed them an eight-second ride if for nothing other than the unconditional support they'd given him since his accident.

Not far from his family, Caitlin sat in the front row. So she was going to watch him compete. He hadn't been sure despite the hug. Gladness filled him, and he felt his mouth break in a wide smile. If she was able to conquer her fears enough to sit through his ride, then maybe they stood a chance. Their gazes connected across the distance and held, convincing Ethan she shared his optimism for their future.

Thirty minutes later, another ten contestants had gone. Ethan liked being one of the last, as it gave him the opportunity to analyze the competition and determine what he needed to do in order to beat their scores. Contestants in jackpots were often weekend enthusiasts and not at the same experience level as those competing professionally.

On the other hand, there was always one or two serious contenders. Ethan studied them the closest.

"Powell, on deck!"

Ethan moved into place beside the chute where Batteries Included waited. As he climbed the fence, the horse twisted and snorted, the whites of his inky-black eyes showing. Ethan swung his good leg over the top rung. The horse kicked out with his front hoof. The clang of iron shoe against metal railing rang out like a challenge, one Ethan accepted.

Muscles clenched, nerves strung tight, he lowered himself onto the bronc's back. Placing his feet in the stirrups, he pointed his toes. Next, he checked the reins and tugged the brim of his hat low over his eyes. When he was satisfied, he whispered a silent prayer to his mother.

One last shift in the saddle, and he uttered the word that could possibly give him back the life he'd lost.

"Go!"

The gate opened. Batteries Included charged into the arena, his powerful body rocking forward and backward with enough strength to jar Ethan's teeth loose.

Acting on pure instinct, he marked the horse. Hand raised over his head, he leaned back in the saddle and found his rhythm.

Time slowed. He heard the roar of air rushing into his expanding lungs, the creak of leather stretching and bending, his bones grinding together, someone hollering his name. He slipped once, righted himself and dug his heels into the horse above the shoulders, urging him to buck higher and harder.

From nowhere, the buzzer sounded.

Ethan's heart exploded. He'd done it!

The pickup men materialized beside him. With a strong arm, the nearest one hauled Ethan out of the saddle and deposited him on the ground. The crowd applauded. Ethan readjusted his hat, dusted off his jeans and began striding across the arena to the gate, his glance repeatedly darting to the scoreboard. Finally, the numbers changed and the announcer's voice blared from the speakers.

"That'll be an 83 for Ethan Powell."

Applause followed. Not wild applause. Ethan had done well enough, though he wouldn't place in the top three. Possibly the top six if he was very, very lucky. Still, it was a decent score for a man with a prosthesis.

Stop thinking like that!

"Good ride." Micky sidled up beside him.

"Not bad."

"You've done worse."

He had. In professional rodeos before he'd enlisted. He'd also done better. A lot better.

"You going to try bull riding again?"

"Probably not." Ethan knew his limits.

"Bareback?"

He'd considered it. Without stirrups he might have even more trouble maintaining his balance. Then again, he might have less. "Soon, I'm thinking."

"Glad to hear it." Micky left to join the other bull riders.

Ethan's buddies congratulated him as he made his way to the pens. Like Micky, they didn't go overboard with their praise. He'd finished, and that was worth acknowledging. Not, he'd finished, and that was an unbelievable accomplishment.

He liked being treated the same as anyone else.

His enjoyment was cut short when the audience gasped loudly. A young man lay prone on the ground. While the pickup men went after the loose horse, wranglers streamed into the arena, surrounding the fallen rider.

The next instant, Caitlin was running pell-mell across the arena, her shoes sinking into the soft dirt. She pushed her way through the wranglers and dropped to the ground, examining the man with expert hands. Not long after, she assisted him to a sitting position, then to his feet. Cheers rose as he limped toward the gate, Caitlin holding his elbow on one side and a wrangler on the other. The announcer wished him well and promised the audience an update on his condition before the jackpot was over.

Returning to work after that was hard for Ethan. He kept thinking about the young man as he supervised the transfer of stock from pens to chutes. News soon spread that the rider had sprained his back. Ethan could easily imagine Caitlin recommending the young man see his regular doctor, and him insisting he was all right. Just as Ethan had done.

He was glad the rider had sprained rather than broken his back. Not only because the injury was less severe. If he'd been driven to the hospital in an ambulance, there would be no convincing Caitlin bronc riding was only moderately dangerous.

Yeah, moderately.

Why was he trying so hard to sway her when she'd insisted there was no chance in hell they'd resume their relationship?

But there had been that hug before he'd competed, and the one at Thanksgiving.

No matter how much she denied it, she liked him. Possibly even loved him, deep down.

He couldn't give up on them.

Two hours later, the Duvall Rodeo Arena's first jackpot came to a close. A brief ceremony followed, and the top three contestants for each event received their belt buckles and winnings. Ethan applauded along with everyone else. He'd rather have been part of the ceremony with Micky and the others.

Soon, he assured himself.

He hung around as long as possible, supervising the wranglers as they returned the remaining livestock to the paddocks and pastures. Every now and then his gaze wandered to the first-aid station. When he saw Caitlin loading up her minivan, he made an excuse to the men and hurried over.

"Need help carrying anything?"

She spun around, nearly dropping the tower of plastic bins in her arms. "Thanks. I've got it."

Not the warm welcome he'd been anticipating after their hug.

"Did you see my ride?" Stupid question. She'd been watching from the bleachers.

"I did." She loaded the plastic bins into her van. "Congratulations. You must be pleased."

"I am."

"Are you celebrating tonight?"

"Hadn't thought of it." He immediately warmed to the idea. "You free? We could have dinner."

She exhaled wearily. "It's been a long day, and I'm exhausted. I'm sure you are, too."

Not really. If anything, he was energized. Had been since his ride.

"Sure. No problem." He hesitated, searching for a reason to stay. "When are you coming out to the ranch next?"

"I'm glad you asked." She brightened, noticeably relieved at the change of topic. "Next Saturday, if that's okay with you."

"Great."

"Any chance we can take the wagon to the park for a test drive? I'd like to experiment with a couple different routes. See which one works best."

"Call me."

No dinner. And a full week before he saw her again. No physical-therapy sessions, either.

So far, this plan he had with Justin to go after his sister was a complete and total bust.

"Good night, Ethan. Congratulations again." She got in her van and left.

As he walked back to the holding pens for a final inspection, he decided he didn't much like being treated the same as every other guy out there.

He much preferred to be special, after all, at least where Caitlin Carmichael was concerned.

Chapter Ten

Caitlin waited at the entrance to the park, shielding her eyes from the brilliant morning sun. She could just make out the wagon with its team of two horses plodding along Mustang Valley's main road at a gentle pace. Vehicles going in both directions slowed at the unusual procession, their drivers used to yielding the right-of-way to horses.

The wagon carried two passengers besides Ethan. Cassie and Isa sat with him on the bench seat, their excited chatter reaching Caitlin's ears from a half block away. Musical tones blended with the girls' voices, and it took Caitlin a moment to recognize the source.

Jingle bells hanging from the harnesses! Ethan must have added them after Caitlin and her crew had finished decorating.

How nice of him.

Guilt needled her with pointy barbs. For the past week, ever since the rodeo jackpot, she'd purposefully avoided Ethan, speaking to him only once midweek to firm up their plans to drive the wagon route before the Holly Days Festival. Evidently he'd gotten her message loud and clear, because he hadn't attempted to contact her, either.

Caitlin should be relieved. Happy, even. Instead, she jumped every time her cell phone rang or the clinic buzzer heralded the arrival of a patient.

This morning was no exception. Her insides fluttered annoyingly at the sight of Ethan's broad shoulders and tall physique, and her palms leaked perspiration.

She wiped them on her jeans, then waved. Only the girls returned her greeting. Was Ethan angry with her for turning down his dinner invitation? As the wagon drew nearer, she noticed Gavin sitting in the bed on a bale of hay and holding on to the sidewall.

Good. More passengers. She'd been a wreck for days, uncertain how she would handle being alone with Ethan. As it turned out, her obsessing had been a complete waste of time.

The horses' clip-clopping hooves on the pavement, the girls' lively chatter and the ringing of jingle bells combined to create a merry cacophony. Caitlin stepped out from her spot beneath an ironwood tree as Ethan expertly turned the horses into the park entrance.

"Whoa, there!" He pulled back on the long reins, and the wagon came to a creaky stop.

Caitlin walked over and gasped softly. "The lights are on!" She hadn't noticed their multicolored flickering in the bright sunlight.

"We're testing the electrical system." Gavin climbed out of the wagon bed, using the rear wheel spokes like a ladder to reach the ground.

Vehicles continued to pass them in a slow procession, the drivers honking or waving. A pickup truck didn't drive past but parked behind the wagon. Caitlin recognized the woman at the wheel. Sage must have followed to prevent potential tailgaters from creeping too close.

The truck door opened and she emerged. "Morning, Caitlin!"

"How are you?"

The two women met up near the wagon. Caitlin liked

Gavin's fiancée and their daughters. Another time and place, she and Sage might have become good friends.

Why not now? a voice inside her asked. *Surely not because of Ethan.*

Avoiding Ethan's family on the off chance he might show up did seem ridiculous. What was the worst that could happen?

Plenty. One smoky glance from him, one caress of his lips on her skin, and she'd be all over him.

Not going to happen, and four co-passengers were the perfect deterrent.

"Come on, girls," Gavin said, climbing out of the wagon. "Let's get a move on."

"You're leaving?"

Caitlin wasn't the only one protesting.

"Aw, Dad, please. Can't we stay with Uncle Ethan?"

Yes, can't they stay?

"We have an appointment," Sage reminded them in a motherly voice. She pulled Caitlin to her for a quick hug. "Maybe after the holidays we can meet for coffee or lunch."

"That would be nice," she mumbled, releasing Sage reluctantly.

The girls continued to whine.

"Tomorrow afternoon I'll take the two of you for another ride," Ethan said. "How's that?"

"Really?" Isa clapped her hands.

"Will you teach to drive?" Cassie asked.

"Yes and yes."

He helped the girls down off the wagon seat into Gavin's outstretched arms, Isa first, then Cassie. They both kissed Ethan's cheek before being lowered, their slim, girlish arms circling his neck.

"Thanks, Uncle Ethan."

"I love you, Uncle Ethan."

"Love you, too, kiddos."

Watching them, Caitlin felt her racing heart slow, then turn to mush. He was incredibly good with the girls, and they seemed to adore him. It had never occurred to her what a terrific father he'd make.

"All aboard!" Gavin beckoned her to the front of the wagon.

"Me?"

"You are riding with Ethan, aren't you?"

She pasted a brave smile on her face. "I am."

"Well, let's do it. Unless you can climb into this wagon by yourself."

Caitlin might be taller than the girls, but she wasn't nearly as nimble. She needed help. Mentally measuring the distance from the ground to the wagon seat, she decided she might need wings.

The footrest was on the same level as her chest. No way could she lift her leg that high.

"Are you kidding me?" She gaped at Gavin.

"Right foot here." He patted one of the wheel spokes. "Left foot here." He tapped the footrest. "Then swing yourself up into the seat."

He made it sound so easy.

The horses chose that moment to shift restlessly, causing the wagon to rock.

Caitlin instinctively drew back. "I can't."

"You'll be fine," Ethan said. "The brake's on."

She wavered, angry at herself. She'd done this before. Granted, that was years ago, when she'd have walked through fire to be with Ethan.

"Okay, okay." She lifted her foot as instructed and placed it on the wheel spoke. Then nothing. Gravity had a hold on her and wouldn't let go.

"Here."

She glanced at Ethan. He'd placed the reins in his left hand and was holding his right one out to her. It was large and strong and appeared more than capable of hauling her safely up into the seat.

"Hang on." Gavin gave her a boost.

She rose up, her left foot automatically seeking purchase. Before she quite knew what was happening, Ethan caught her by the forearm and yanked. Her world tilted crazily. Then she was seated beside him, and everything returned to its proper place.

It had been like that before, when they were young. He had only to touch her, hold her, and all was right once more.

"It's high up here." Higher than she remembered. Her fingers gripped the thin and unreassuring metal armrest. "No seat belts, huh?" She laughed nervously.

"I don't remember you being so afraid of horses."

She hadn't been, only since Justin's accident. She hadn't been afraid of fast cars, roller coasters, bungee jumping or heights before then, either.

"I haven't ridden for years."

"We should go one day. Get you used to horses again."

"Get me used to the wagon first. Then we'll see about horses."

"One step at a time." Before she could wonder if he was really talking about them, he said, "Molly and Dolly are the two calmest horses on the ranch next to Chico. I wouldn't take you or anyone for a drive if I thought for one second we'd have a runaway."

Runaway! Why had he mentioned that? "How reliable is that brake?"

She immediately imagined the horses galloping hell-bent for election through the park like in those old black-and-white Westerns she used to watch as a kid.

As it turned out, she'd panicked for nothing. The horses,

under Ethan's careful guidance, traveled along at a sedate walk. After several minutes, Caitlin started breathing again. Before long, she relaxed enough to appreciate the advantages her elevated position offered. She had a clear view of the workers erecting the miniature Santa's workshop and the obedience trials under way in the dog park across the expansive green. In the far distance, Pinnacle Peak, with its distinctive silhouette, reached skyward as if to capture the sun.

"How beautiful."

Ethan smiled, and they drove for a while in companionable silence.

Eventually, Caitlin pulled a map of the park from her pocket. "I figured we'd have the wagon pickup and drop-off station near the picnic area, next to the Santa's workshop."

He grunted approvingly.

"We could set up a table here—" she tapped the map "—and take donations for the mustang sanctuary. Pass out literature if you have any."

He grunted again.

"Do you think Cassie would be willing to dress in an elf costume and be one of Santa's helpers?"

"Probably."

When he said no more, Caitlin continued examining the map and the routes she'd sketched out. "What do you think about this one?" She angled the map for him to see.

He grumbled instead of grunting.

Fine. He was keeping conversation to a minimum. That suited her, as well. Folding the map, she returned it to her pocket, sat back and kept quiet.

For two full minutes.

"Did I do something to upset you?"

"Not at all."

"I'm sorry about refusing your dinner invitation last Saturday. I figured it was better if we—"

"You're not going to give me the let's-be-friends speech, are you?"

Her cheeks burned. That was exactly what she'd been planning. "No. Don't be ridiculous."

"Because I won't be friends with you."

That stung.

"I want more."

"More?" Her voice sounded small.

"Much more."

Oh, dear.

"Look at me, Caitlin."

She did, tensing as his smoldering gaze raked over her.

"Don't expect me to make small talk with you when what I really want is to make love."

"I'm sorry." Caitlin sucked in air, then released it in a shuddering breath.

"Don't be. I'm not propositioning you, simply stating a fact."

She and Ethan were no strangers to intimacy. They had been each other's firsts, consummating their love shortly after high school graduation. The night had been one of the scariest of her life, and the most memorable. Scary for Ethan, too. Revealing his true feelings had endeared him to her and broken down the last of her defenses. When she gave herself to him, it was without reservation and without regrets.

Magic had happened that night and for many nights afterward. Making love with Ethan had been extraordinary. Fulfilling, satisfying and fun. But physical pleasure—and there had been a lot of it—was never more important than their emotional connection, which only grew stronger the longer they were together.

Yet another reason why his abrupt enlistment in the marines had devastated her. How could he have loved her so completely and so thoroughly and then abandoned her like that?

The horses plodded along the side street circling the park, the sleigh bells chiming in rhythm to the cadence of their hooves.

Seconds ticked by, then minutes.

"Was there anybody after me?" Caitlin was shocked at her own audacity.

Ethan answered without pause. "I dated some in the marines."

"No one special?"

"No one I fell in love with." He clucked to Molly and Dolly, who had stopped at the sight of an elderly couple walking a shaggy terrier.

"What about since your discharge?"

"Haven't had the time."

Was that true? Or did the loss of his leg have something to do with it?

Justin had been painfully shy around girls as a teenager, frequently becoming tongue-tied. After his accident, he'd refused to even be alone in the same room with someone of the opposite sex.

Not anymore, Caitlin mused, remembering him and Tamiko together.

When had Justin changed? And what had prompted it?

"How about you?" Ethan's sidelong glance gave nothing away. "Date much?"

"Not hardly at all until after college. Caring for Justin took up most of my free time. And then there was homework and work-study programs. I met someone a few years ago."

"Tell me about him."

He wasn't you. The thought came from nowhere and traveled straight to her chest, where it curled around her heart.

Caitlin averted her head to hide the tears that sprang unbidden to her eyes.

"We went out for about two years," she said when she'd composed herself. "Then it just kind of fizzled. No big fight. No drama. We parted friends."

"Too bad."

What she didn't tell Ethan was that her boyfriend had wanted to marry her, and had repeatedly proposed. Caitlin couldn't bring herself to take the next step—because of Ethan or Justin or both, she really wasn't sure. Eventually, her boyfriend grew tired of waiting. There'd been no one since, not even a casual date. Which also meant that Ethan's kiss at the rodeo arena was her first one in years.

"I thought maybe we'd have the wagon rides on Friday and Saturday nights only," she said. "From six to nine." The small talk sounded trite after such a personal conversation. "Is that too long? I don't want to tire the horses."

"I'll have two teams. One for each night."

"Will you take the other team out for a test run, too?"

"Tomorrow. With the girls. Want to come along?" He studied her face intently.

Were there tearstains on her cheeks? She instinctively touched them. Dry, thank goodness.

"I, um, promised Mom I'd go Christmas shopping with her."

If she didn't already have a legitimate excuse, she would have manufactured one. Her resistance to him was at an all-time low. It would be so easy to say she didn't care about his bronc riding, scoot closer and rest her head on his shoulder.

"You having Christmas Day at your place?" he asked.

"Oh, gosh, no!"

"Condo too small?"

"That, and too empty."

"Still moving in?"

"I've been waiting to see if I'm…" *staying in Mustang Valley* "…keeping the condo. I don't have one Christmas decoration up or one card displayed. Mom and Dad are having dinner at their house. My aunt and uncle and cousin are driving up from Green Valley. Some friends from Dad's work will also be there."

"You'll have fun."

"Is Sierra coming home?"

"She hasn't committed one way or the other." Ethan absently clucked to the horses. "I don't know what's with her lately. She's cut herself off from the family almost completely. Dad's pretty upset."

"Is it a man?"

"I hadn't thought of that."

"Getting involved in a relationship is one reason people ignore their families and friends."

"Why wouldn't she tell us?"

"Maybe she's afraid you won't approve of him."

Ethan stared at the road, his jaw working.

"I'm not saying it's a man. Could be anything."

"It makes sense, though."

Caitlin left Ethan to his thoughts, concentrating instead on her own. When they rounded the last bend on the route, the towering Christmas tree the Holly Days committee had erected in the center of the park came into view. Caitlin felt a sentimental tug on her heartstrings. This was her favorite season.

"If you could have just one wish for Christmas," she asked, "what would it be?"

Ethan didn't immediately answer. She assumed he was thinking of Sierra and his bronc riding. Of his desire to compete professionally. His job training horses. Her, and his desire for them to get back together.

"That was a silly question," she blurted when the silence stretched. "You don't have to answer it."

"What I'd want most of all is for things to go back the way they were. Before my mother got sick and we were still raising cattle."

Ten years ago she and Ethan had been planning a wedding in the not-too-distant future. Ten years ago, he had yet to enlist.

"But that isn't possible." He shook the reins. If the horses were supposed to walk faster, they didn't pay attention. "So, I guess I'd wish for the riding stables to do well and Gavin's stud and breeding business to take off. He's trying hard to preserve what little we have left in order to pass it down to his children."

A noble, selfless wish. "What about you, Ethan? What do *you* want?"

He turned his head, the ghost of a smile lighting his lips. "For us, you and me, to be happy. And I don't mean together, necessarily," he added, as if anticipating her objection.

No?

Neither of them had been happy apart.

"I'd like that, too," she said softly, realizing it was her Christmas wish, as well.

ETHAN WALKED THE PERIMETER of the last stall in the nearly completed mare motel. "Looking good."

"I agree." Gavin nodded approvingly.

The crew had finished hanging the twenty-four stall doors an hour earlier, shortly after Ethan returned home from his ride with Caitlin. While there was a long punch list needing completion, and minor modifications here and there, the mare motel was operational and ready for "guests."

"If I hadn't seen it myself," Clay said, his deep voice resonating with awe and admiration, "I wouldn't have believed this was once a cattle barn."

Indeed, the transformation was nothing short of amazing. Ethan could hardly remember what the barn had looked like in "the old days," as his niece was fond of saying—the remark accompanied by an eye roll.

A wave of nostalgia overcame him, bringing with it memory after memory. He, Gavin and Conner had spent considerable time in this cattle barn while growing up. Working, not playing. Wayne Powell had been a taskmaster, requiring his sons to give one-hundred-and-ten percent. They hadn't really appreciated his strict work ethic until they were adults.

Clay had worked alongside them on occasion, when he wasn't busy with his father's cattle operation. Back then, the future had seemed both certain and endless. Gavin would take over the family business. Ethan would run it with him, after winning a world championship at the National Rodeo Finals. And Sierra would marry a local boy—Conner, possibly—and move to a house just down the road. The three siblings would produce a passel of rascally children to try their parents and entertain their grandparents.

It hadn't turned out that way. All things considered, their lives weren't so bad.

"Mom would be proud," Ethan mused out loud as he, Gavin and Clay strode down the bright and airy aisle.

"She would," Gavin agreed.

Clay smiled fondly. "When is Camelot Farms arriving with their mares?"

The farm's half-Arabian, half-quarter-horse animals would be the first to reside in the mare motel.

"In the morning," Gavin answered.

"How many are they bringing?"

"Just two."

Gavin hoped to keep all twenty-four stalls filled. Unfortunately, a stud and breeding business took months, if not years, to establish. Prince had proved himself capable of impregnating mares, as a recent veterinarian exam had confirmed. But it wasn't enough. His foals had to be born healthy, inherit their sire's best qualities, then grow into fine horses. Only then would customers beat down the Powells' door.

Patience was required, and Gavin's was in short supply.

Even now, as he stared at the cooling fans suspended from the barn ceiling, he seemed distracted. More than once Ethan or Clay had to repeat themselves because Gavin wasn't listening.

"Anything in the bunkhouse the men need to finish before I send them home?" Clay asked.

"Nope." Like the cattle barn, Ethan's bunkhouse barely resembled its former incarnation. During the past two weeks, the workers had pushed hard. "They finished constructing the built-in bookcases yesterday."

"You buy an automatic coffeemaker yet?"

"Very funny." He had bought one, but he wasn't about to tell Clay. The bunkhouse, now an apartment, suited him fine without making accommodations for anyone.

Except for Caitlin.

He'd be willing to change his bachelor ways, and pad, for her. Make concessions. Alter his habits. Compromise.

He wasn't willing to give up bronc riding and breaking green horses.

Until then, there was no point even imagining sharing living quarters with her.

"Gavin," Clay said. "Gavin!"

Ethan jerked. His brother wasn't the only one who was distracted.

"Yeah." Gavin blinked as if orienting himself. "What?"

"I asked where the backup generator is located."

"Nowhere for now. We need to decide, and hook it up."

"You okay?"

"Fine." Gavin grinned stupidly.

"You're not acting fine."

"I'm preoccupied." His stupid grin grew even wider.

Ethan couldn't recall seeing his brother act like that, other than the day he'd proposed to Sage. "Is there something you're not telling us?"

"No." Gavin shook his head, then laughed. "Yes."

"Which is it?"

"I'm not supposed to say anything."

"Sage is bred," Clay uttered bluntly.

Leave it to a cattleman to use animal vernacular when describing a pregnancy.

"Is she?" Ethan felt his own mouth stretch into a smile.

"She took the home pregnancy test this morning. We'd planned on waiting before having a baby. A year at least."

"Congratulations." Ethan pumped his brother's hand, then captured him in a headlock. "Dad's going to be thrilled."

"Don't say anything," Gavin warned, after enduring a suffocating hug from Clay. "I promised Sage. She wants to wait until she sees the doctor."

"Let's celebrate," Clay suggested. "Lunch at the Rusty Nail. My treat."

The local saloon and grill had been one of their favorite hangouts in years past.

"I'm in."

"Call Conner. Maybe he can cut loose from work and join us."

An hour later, the four friends were seated at a table, having beer with their hamburgers and reminiscing about their high school years and all the trouble they'd managed to get into.

Gavin didn't stop smiling, except when he talked about Sage or Cassie. Then his expression grew soft and his voice low. Ethan was truly happy for his brother. He was also jealous and wouldn't mind having a little happiness for himself.

With Caitlin.

Ethan couldn't see himself loving and living with any other woman but her, which explained why he'd dated only occasionally since they'd broken up.

Caitlin wasn't his better half, she was his *other* half. The piece of him that had been missing for years.

Maybe he should consider quitting busting broncs. After the jackpot last week, everyone knew he could still ride with the big boys.

He toyed with the idea of giving up his lifelong dream, and to his shock and alarm, it no longer frightened the hell out of him.

Chapter Eleven

Caitlin stood in line behind a dad and his pair of preschoolers. The girl, the older of the two, wriggled excitedly and chattered incessantly. The boy wore a solemn expression and chewed nervously on the tip of his mitten.

"Look at the horses!" The girl grasped her brother by the shoulders and shook him. "Real horses."

Caitlin decided the family must not be from Mustang Valley. Most of the residents owned horses, had neighbors with horses or rented them at the Powells' stables. They wouldn't get that excited over the prospect of seeing "real" ones. As she glanced around, it occurred to her there were quite a number of unfamiliar faces at the Holly Days Festival. Articles in the local newspapers and advertisements on radio stations must have attracted people from all over the Phoenix metropolitan area.

A moment later, the man finished his transaction with Sage. "Come on, kids," he said.

The girl skipped alongside him as they headed to the decorated wagon. The boy lagged behind. Caitlin was convinced he would be as enthused as his sister by the time they returned from their ride. She didn't see how much money the dad had given Sage as a donation, but her cheery, "Thank you so much and Merry Christmas," led Caitlin to believe the amount was generous.

"How's business?" she asked, stepping up to the folding table that was serving as a ticket counter. Tamiko had painted a large poster advertising the wagon rides and the mustang sanctuary, and had taped it to the front of the table.

"Couldn't be better!" Sage gushed. "Most people are giving more than what we're asking for the tickets."

"I'm so glad."

"This was a fantastic idea you had. I can't thank you enough for getting the committee to agree."

"We couldn't have done it without Ethan and his family." Caitlin glanced over at him. Ethan sat in the wagon with his back to her, but they'd exchanged looks often during the evening, each one giving her a small tingle. "The festival is everything we had hoped it would be, and they're a big reason why."

During the past week, the stately pine tree in the center of the park had been decorated with silver and gold ornaments and candy canes. The white lights strung through its boughs flickered merrily. Santa's workshop, complete with artificial snow, a replica North Pole and a life-size Rudolph the Red-nosed Reindeer, had been erected across from the tree. Santa sat on a makeshift throne, his pudgy belly hanging over his belt, his white beard covering his chest. The line of children waiting to have their pictures taken with him extended clear to the back of the workshop.

Cassie and Isa, dressed in elf costumes, complete with fake pointed ears, assisted Mrs. Claus with crowd control.

"I still can't believe how many people are here." Caitlin stepped aside to let another customer purchase tickets from Sage.

"There'll be a lot more tomorrow night, I bet."

The festival was scheduled for a full three days, as long as the weather held, which the forecasts predicted it would. Friday night, all day Saturday, and Sunday till four.

Caitlin couldn't be more pleased with the attendance and the positive feedback she'd been receiving. The hard work of the various committee members and crews of energetic volunteers was paying off.

"Excuse me." A woman leaned around Caitlin. "Four tickets, please."

"This wagon is full," Sage apologized with a bright smile. "You'll have to wait for the next ride, in about half an hour."

"How's Ethan holding up?" Caitlin asked Sage when the woman left, tickets for the next ride clutched in her gloved fist.

"You haven't talked to him tonight?"

"Not yet."

Caitlin didn't admit she'd seen him only once since the previous weekend, when he'd taken her for a drive in the wagon, and that was for a PT session. Nor did she admit how much he'd been on her mind. It seemed for a while there they'd been seeing each other every few days. Lately, hardly at all.

She missed him.

A small part of her wondered if she'd acted too hastily when she'd told him there was no chance for a reconciliation.

"He's fine," Sage said. "Though I bet he'll be exhausted by tomorrow night. Driving a wagon is more tiring than you might think, and it takes hours and hours to get ready. He's been at it since noon. Grooming the horses. Cleaning the harnesses. He even washed and ironed his shirt." She winked at Caitlin. "I like a man who does his own laundry."

"Is his shoulder holding up?"

"He hasn't complained."

"He wouldn't."

"You're right about that. He's still doing his exercises, or so he says."

"That's good."

"Where'd all the customers go?" Sage glanced around. "Oh, well." She used the lull to transfer money from the cash box to a press-and-seal plastic bag. "If I give you my keys, would you mind running this to my truck for me? It's in the parking lot. I don't like sitting here with all this cash."

"Glad to," Caitlin said. The stack of bills Sage stuffed in the bag, mostly small denominations, was three inches thick. "Wow, that is a lot of money."

"I'm hoping by the end of the weekend we'll have enough collected to bring two mustangs down from the Bureau of Land Management facility in Show Low. Our first foster horses for the sanctuary."

"Are they injured?" Caitlin tucked the bag of money inside her jacket and out of sight.

"Only superficial wounds sustained during the roundup."

Caitlin really didn't have a reason to stick around talking to Sage, other than she enjoyed the company. She just couldn't bring herself to leave while the wagon was still parked at the corner.

While Ethan was nearby.

As she watched, he clucked to Molly and Dolly and set out amid whoops and cheers from his passengers, the sleigh bells jingling and the lights blinking.

Caitlin attempted a smile, but her mouth wouldn't cooperate.

What was wrong with her?

Sage paid no attention and continued prattling on about the foster mustangs.

"These two horses are what the BLM considers unadoptable. Even with a reduced price of twenty-five dollars each, no one would purchase them."

"Why? Are they mean?"

"No, just wild and not adapting to confinement. But they're so beautiful and spirited. I'm convinced, with the right training, they can make really nice horses for someone. Ethan's skills will be tested for sure."

"He'll train them?"

Of course he would, Caitlin thought, answering her own question. He broke rodeo stock for Clay and green horses for the Powells' clients.

"He did a fantastic job with Prince," Sage declared. "You won't believe how well that horse is doing. You should come out to the ranch and see him."

"Prince wasn't unadoptable."

"He was wild," Sage explained. "Living in the mountains. You can't get much more unadoptable than that."

"If these mustangs aren't adapting, are you sure it's safe for Ethan to try and train them?"

"As if I could keep him away."

As if anyone could. Certainly not Caitlin.

...when what I really want to do is make love to you.

How often had she heard him say that in her head this past week?

What would it be like making love with him now? she wondered. Different from when they were younger, certainly. They weren't the same people anymore.

Discovering the changes would be interesting. Exciting. Thrilling.

Enough was enough. She wasn't getting back together with Ethan, and she definitely wasn't going to have sex with him.

She patted the bank bag inside her jacket. "I'll put this in your truck and be right back."

"No hurry."

While Caitlin was crossing the parking lot, she glimpsed the wagon with its multicolored lights and excited passengers. It was a charming sight, one straight off the front of a Christmas card.

Ethan really was working his tail off for the committee. For *her*.

She should do something for him, she decided. A token of appreciation.

Nothing personal. It wasn't as if she was trying to bridge the distance that had developed between them.

When she returned to the table, Clay was there. Caitlin arrived just as he was pulling Sage out of her chair and into his arms.

"Congratulations," he boomed.

She laughed and pushed him away. "Who told you?"

"Who do you think?"

"What's going on?" Caitlin asked, her interest piqued.

"Nothing." Sage took the keys from Caitlin's outstretched hand, her cheeks flushed a deep crimson and her eyes sparkling.

"Come on. Something's up. Tell me."

"Tell her," Clay coaxed. "You know you want to."

Sage sighed. "I was going to make an appointment at the clinic next week, so I suppose you'd have found out eventually."

"You're pregnant!" Caitlin guessed.

"Not so loud." Sage placed a finger to her lips. "I haven't told Isa yet."

"I'm so happy for you!" Caitlin reached across the table and clasped Sage's hands in hers.

"We were going to wait. It was an accident."

"The best kind of accident."

They didn't have much time to talk because a large group of Red Hat ladies descended upon them. Clay convinced the women to add another ten dollars to their donation.

When they left, Sage asked him, "How's that cowboy who got hurt?"

"Better."

Caitlin stilled. "Who got hurt?"

"Micky Lannon," Clay said.

"Micky?" The father of the little girl with the cut knee. "What happened?" she demanded.

"He got bucked off last night."

"From a horse?"

"A bull." Clay and Caitlin continued their conversation while Sage passed out flyers. "Broke his leg in three places. They had to operate this morning, insert some pins. I just came from the hospital. He's going to be released tomorrow."

"Poor guy." Caitlin pressed her hands to her cheeks. "How's his wife holding up?"

"All right, I think."

"What about his job?"

"He's taking a medical leave of absence. Six to eight weeks."

Caitlin wished she had been there to help. Unfortunately, Clay had hired her only for jackpots and rodeo events, not regular practices. There probably wasn't much she could have done anyway. Not with a break that severe.

"What about health insurance?"

"He has it."

Even with coverage, there would be costs. Hefty costs. And he'd be out of work almost two months, which would put a strain on his family and finances. He should have thought of that before climbing on a bull.

"The men are taking up a collection for him. Didn't Ethan tell you?"

Why did everyone think she and Ethan spoke on a regular basis?

"No. I haven't seen him recently." Even if she had, she doubted he'd have mentioned Micky's fall, knowing how upset she'd get.

"Can I interest you two lovely ladies in a hot chocolate?" Clay asked.

"Mmm." Sage rubbed her palms together. "Yes, please. It's getting chilly."

Caitlin was so engrossed in her thoughts she barely noticed Clay leaving.

Her mind raced. It could have easily been Ethan in the hospital, recovering from a serious surgery. Her chest constricted at the image of him lying with his leg—his one good leg—elevated in a fiberglass cast.

She couldn't bear it if he was hurt like that.

A moan of distress involuntarily escaped her lips.

"Caitlin? You okay?"

She looked over to discover Sage staring at her, a curious expression on her face.

"You're here!" Caitlin hurried over to Justin and her parents. She'd spotted them in the parking lot while making yet another money run to Sage's truck. "I wasn't sure you'd make it."

"Sorry, I got stuck at the office." Her dad slung his arms around Caitlin and her mother. "How soon till the festival closes?"

"Nine."

He whistled. "Doesn't give us much time."

The lateness of the hour and the dropping temperature had no effect on the crowd. People were still arriving in droves.

"Is Tamiko here?" Justin asked, wheeling along beside Caitlin.

That didn't take long.

"Yes. But so is what's-his-name."

What *was* his name? Eric, right?

The presence of Tamiko's boyfriend didn't appear to deter Justin. "Hook up with you later," he said, and was gone.

"Who is this Tamiko?" Caitlin's mother asked in a concerned tone. "He hasn't mentioned her before."

"One of my volunteers. They met at the ranch when we were decorating the wagon."

Typical father, her dad asked, "Is she pretty?"

Typical mother, her mom asked, "Is she nice?"

"Both." Caitlin laughed. "And she likes Justin."

There was just the matter of that pesky boyfriend.

The three of them strolled to the festival grounds. Caitlin often marveled at how easily her parents had adjusted to her brother's loss of mobility and independent lifestyle. Sure, they had worried when he was first injured. And periodically in the years since, especially when he moved away from home and into his own apartment. But never for long, it seemed.

Caitlin was the one who fretted. The one who couldn't cut the apron strings.

Then again, she was the one consumed with guilt over Justin's paralysis. How could her parents, knowing the part she'd played, love her as they did, forgive her as they had?

Justin, too.

Her mother stopped to take everything in. "Are the wagon rides still going on?"

"There's one more at least, maybe two."

"We'd better hurry and buy our tickets." She was off, leaving Caitlin and her father in the dust.

When they reached the table, Caitlin's dad purchased the last two tickets and gave a very large donation that had Sage practically in tears. "Thank you, Mr. Carmichael. Mrs. Carmichael. Can I add you to our list of newsletter subscribers?"

Caitlin could tell one more foster mustang would be arriving from Show Low.

"Too bad Justin's going to miss out," Caitlin's mother mused. "He'd enjoy the wagon ride."

"He's going," Sage said brightly. "He bought a ticket right before you."

"Wonderful."

No, it wasn't.

Apparently Caitlin was the only one who wondered how he'd get up into the wagon without a lift, and how embarrassing it might be for him with all these strangers watching.

"Doug, let's check out the craft tables while we're waiting." Her mother latched on to her husband's arm.

"Send a search party if we're not back in three days," he called to Caitlin.

"Any chance I can recruit you to help me tomorrow night?" Sage asked as they walked away.

"Sure. I was planning on being here, anyway."

Ten minutes later, the wagon returned from its run, the passengers singing Christmas carols. By the time Ethan reined the horses to a stop at the drop-off point, dozens more people milling nearby had joined in with the carolers.

Cheer spread from person to person, carried by a smile.

Caitlin felt her own mouth curve up at the corners. She had spent considerable effort and energy working on the festival. This was, however, the first moment she'd felt truly touched by the Christmas spirit.

She sought out Ethan. He must have sensed her gaze on him because he turned and looked at her…and kept looking. The warmth within her that had started with the caroling continued to build.

Ethan was responsible for this wondrous night. She'd asked for his help and, as always, he'd given it. Unconditionally. Even during the past couple weeks when she'd been avoiding him as much as possible.

She wanted to give him a gift of appreciation—and affection. And suddenly she knew just what it would be.

"We'd better hurry." Caitlin's mother carried three plastic

sacks, last-minute Christmas purchases from the craft tables. "Where on earth is Justin?"

The passengers had stopped singing and were climbing down from the wagon one by one, their faces radiant. They exchanged greetings with people lining up for the next ride.

"Here he comes," Caitlin's dad said.

She saw her brother wheeling toward them. Tamiko walked beside him. They made a striking couple, Justin with his fair complexion, Tamiko with her long black hair and exotic beauty.

Not a couple, Caitlin reminded herself.

Where was her boyfriend, Eric?

"Who's this?" her mother asked when Justin and Tamiko joined them in line, even though Caitlin had already told her.

Tamiko put out her hand. "Hi. I'm Justin's friend Tamiko."

Justin's friend? Not, Caitlin thought, one of the festival volunteers.

"Nice to meet you." Caitlin's mother's eyes were bright with curiosity. "Do you attend ASU, too?"

Justin stared at Tamiko with such raw longing, Caitlin couldn't bring herself to watch them. He'd get hurt if he wasn't careful, and there was nothing she or anyone could do to prevent it.

"You coming, honey?" her father asked.

"I didn't buy a ticket."

"They won't charge you. Not with all the work you've put in."

She could always give Sage a donation tomorrow night. And the wagon ride would be fun. "Sure, why not?"

Caitlin and her family fell into line. The wagon, with its hay bale seats, could easily accommodate ten people and two or three small children sitting on laps. Another person, usually an older child or teenager, rode shotgun next to Ethan.

While the passengers boarded, he stood, stretched and

rolled his bad shoulder. It must have been an arduous day for him.

Justin wheeled to the rear of the wagon and waited for a woman with incredibly inappropriate stilettos to be hoisted up by her husband.

Caitlin had to intervene. "Dad, are you going to help Justin?"

"If he asks me."

"Aren't you concerned how he'll get in the wagon?"

"Not as much as you are."

She grumbled to herself. They could possibly fit the wheelchair into the bed if a bale of hay was removed. That would require a pair of strong arms.

"You first," Justin told Tamiko.

"Hey, what gives?" Her boyfriend abruptly stepped in front of them. Had he been there all along? "He's not riding with us."

"Yes, he is," Tamiko answered coolly.

"I bought a ticket, dude." Justin held up an orange stub.

"Yeah? Well, news flash, *dude*. No room for your wheels."

"I'm not hooked to this chair by wires," Justin said with a chuckle.

Caitlin willed herself not to say anything. She'd interfered before, only to incur her brother's anger. He insisted on fighting his own battles.

Her parents didn't appear to be concerned. They watched their son closely but made no move in his direction.

"Come on, Tamiko." Her boyfriend snatched her hand.

"What about Justin?"

"You heard him. He's not hooked to that chair."

The other passengers had all boarded and were watching the scene unfolding before them with rabid interest.

"This is better than reality TV," one woman said.

The hell with making Justin mad. Caitlin had reached her limit. "Okay, guys—"

"Stay out of it," her father ordered.

"Dad!"

"I mean it, honey."

"I'm not leaving Justin," Tamiko said stubbornly.

"You'd pick him over me?" Eric demanded.

"We're friends. Why can't you be nice?"

"This is stupid." Caitlin took a step forward.

A large, strong hand on her arm pulled her back. She pivoted, intending to tell her father they should—

It wasn't her dad restraining her. It was Ethan.

"Let me handle this," he said, and brushed past her.

Caitlin started to follow.

"Young lady!" Her father's stern voice stopped her in her tracks. "What did I tell you? Butt out."

"Dammit," she grumbled. Why did she have to butt out and not Ethan?

He walked over to Justin. "You ready?"

"If you are."

A look of understanding passed between them.

Ethan bent down and placed one arm beneath Justin's legs and the other behind his back. He lifted her brother out of the chair and carried him the short distance to the wagon. Another man sitting on a hay bale jumped up. Without being asked, he took Justin from Ethan and gently deposited him on the nearest empty seat. The three of them worked together so smoothly, they might have done this before.

And just like that, it was over.

Caitlin's father helped her mother and then Tamiko into the wagon. Her boyfriend clambered up after her, scowling as he squeezed by Justin.

"You coming, honey?"

"Yeah, Dad."

Ethan appeared next to her. "You can sit with me if you want."

She turned to her father, but he was already halfway in the wagon. "I guess I will."

Conner sat in the seat, holding the reins, while T.J. gripped Dolly's bridle. The two cowboys had been helping Ethan with the horses all night.

Ethan climbed up first. Once he had hold of the reins, Conner jumped down. Molly and Dolly, tired after their long night, didn't so much as twitch an ear.

Ethan held out a hand to Caitlin.

She tried to remember where to place her feet. Wheel spoke left? Footrest right?

"Need help?" Conner didn't wait for an answer, and gave her a boost.

By some miracle, she made it into the seat, clumsily plopping down beside Ethan. Before she was quite settled he clucked to the horses and they were off.

She glanced over her shoulder at her brother. He appeared fine. Not the least bit self-conscious. He seemed to be enjoying himself, talking with the man who'd helped him. Smiling at Tamiko.

Such a change from the shy, geeky kid he'd been.

If Caitlin hadn't encouraged him to go to the river that day, it might have been him sitting next to Tamiko. Taking her to a dance. Walking with her down a church aisle one day.

"He's all right," Ethan said.

"I was checking on my parents."

"Liar."

She sighed. "Am I that transparent?"

"Only to those of us who know you well."

He did know her well, and she him. Which made this

game they were playing—drawing toward each other, then stepping back—all the more frustrating.

"Thanks for helping Justin out."

"He's a good kid."

"Yeah, he is. And I'm sure he appreciates what you did for him." She bit her lower lip, worrying it between her teeth. "So do I," she finally admitted.

His reply was a simple, "You're welcome."

"I apologize for the mixed messages I've been sending you."

"Maybe they weren't so mixed."

Maybe they weren't.

A tiny sliver of awareness arrowed through her.

"I'm here for you, Caitlin, and I'm willing to wait. For however long it takes."

That wasn't what he'd said before. He'd left on a whim, broken her heart.

Could she trust him again?

Perhaps the more important question was, did she want to live the rest of her life without him?

Chapter Twelve

"Isa, come back here!" Sage muttered an expletive in Spanish under her breath. Jumping down from the wagon, she chased her daughter across the green to the Santa's workshop.

"Just think," Ethan ribbed Gavin, who sat on the seat beside him. "Soon you and Sage will have another kid to wear you down and teach you a second language."

"Yeah." His brother grinned, something he'd been doing a lot lately. "I can't wait."

None of the Powells could. Sage's resolve had weakened yet again, and this morning she'd broken the news of her pregnancy to the rest of the family. The girls had squealed with excitement. Ethan's father had cried.

"By the way, you're going to have to buy a new suit," Gavin said. "We're moving up the wedding date from May to February. Sage doesn't want to be fat as a cow in her wedding dress. Her words," he added emphatically, "not mine."

"Can you pull everything together by then?"

"I think so. If we keep it casual and simple."

"Let me know what you need help with."

"Consider yourself on notice." Gavin swung out of the seat, landing easily on the ground.

"Clay can be in charge of the bachelor party."

Gavin moaned. "Whatever you do, don't tell Sage." He headed to the horses to check on them.

Ethan chuckled. He was glad for his brother.

Six months ago, the Powells were barely making ends meet, and their future looked bleak. Gavin had believed it was entirely up to him to put their riding stables in the black. He'd done it, with a little help from the rest of the family and good friends, including Clay. He'd also gained a fiancée and stepdaughter in the process.

Quite an accomplishment for a man who, until recently, considered himself unmarriageable and a poor excuse for a father.

Ethan held a similar opinion of himself. Though lately, with the help of Cassie and Isa, he was learning how to be a good uncle. That was a start.

"Isa forgot her hat." Cassie, in full elf costume, held up a striped stocking cap with an enormous tassel on the end.

She, Isa and Sage had ridden in the bed of the wagon from the ranch, while Ethan's father followed in the truck. He and Gavin had been tapped to help Ethan tonight with the horses.

"Come on, Dad." Cassie scrambled out of the wagon. "I'll show you and Grandpa Santa's workshop."

"You okay alone for a bit?" Gavin asked Ethan.

"Go on. Have fun."

The pair met up with Ethan's dad on his walk over from the parking lot.

All the Powells were together for an outing. Ethan didn't have to search his memory for the last time that had happened. He remembered it clearly—Fourth of July fireworks, right before his mother's body rejected the donor heart, and she succumbed to infection.

He'd taken Caitlin to the fireworks display, naturally, and they'd kissed under the brilliantly lit sky, pledging their love and devotion. No wonder she was still angry at him. If she had up and left him shortly after a night like that, he'd have trouble forgiving her.

She would be here tonight, helping Sage sell tickets and take donations. Ethan intended to get her alone at some point before the evening ended. A small wrapped package was burning a hole in his jacket pocket, and he was eager to give it to her. The gift wouldn't make up for all the grief and misery he'd caused her, but he hoped she would see the meaning behind it and think a little better of him.

One of the horses lowered his head and pawed the pavement, more ready than his buddy to get started.

Ethan had brought a different team tonight. They weren't as nicely matched as Dolly and Molly, but equally dependable. The geldings had been full of energy when they left the ranch. A two-mile walk down the long road had tired them out some, and by their third trip around the park, they'd be beat.

So would Ethan. He hadn't worked this hard since basic training, but he'd do it again in a heartbeat if Caitlin asked him.

Ethan noticed her then, taking the same route as his father from the parking lot across the green. She carried a large tote bag pressed close to her side, as if the contents were fragile or precious.

Caitlin went straight to the table, waving briefly to him, and seemed perplexed to find no one there. She looked around, set her tote bag down, then picked it up again.

He'd have gone over to talk to her if he could leave the horses. Instead, he imagined her coming to him.

In the next moment she did, wearing a radiant smile.

She aimed it at him, and he swore they were back at the fireworks display, sitting beneath the brilliantly lit sky.

Before she reached him, his father and Gavin met up with her. She gave his dad a hug and a kiss on the cheek. Ethan was jealous. Gavin received the same treatment, and Ethan was even more jealous. He was seriously considering leaping down from the wagon and collecting his kiss and hug when she came to stand by him, her hand resting on the wheel.

"Hey."

"Can I interest you in a ride, ma'am?"

"Maybe later." She laughed softly and transformed once more into the old Caitlin. They were young, flirting outrageously and unable to get enough of each other. "I promised I'd help Sage tonight."

"The supplies are in the truck," Wayne said. "If you're looking for them."

"I'll wait for Sage." She shrugged, causing her tote bag to slip. She hefted the straps back onto her shoulder, running her fingers tentatively down the side.

"She might be a while. I can fetch them for you."

"Do you mind? I'll go with you."

Ethan saw his opportunity and grabbed it. "I'll do it. Gavin, get over here and watch these horses for me."

"Did you want to leave your stuff here?" Ethan asked. "Dad will watch it."

"No." Caitlin hugged the tote closer. "That's all right."

They walked side by side, though not close and not touching. Small talk came easy.

"Are you ready for Christmas?"

Her question reminded Ethan they'd seen little of each other lately.

"Me? No. I'm a last-minute shopper." He thought of the gift in his pocket. "Usually. But Sage and the girls have transformed the house. There's a tree in the living room, a wreath on the front door and cookies baking in the oven every day. Dad's trying to set some kind of record."

"Sounds wonderful."

"It is." The preparations took him back to when he was a kid and his mother had gone all-out for Christmas with the same gusto as Sage and the rest of his family. "What about you?"

"I've finished my shopping."

"More than I can say."

"Still haven't done anything with the condo or even sent out one card. I'm so bad."

"You're busy."

"Not that busy."

"By the way, Clay's having another jackpot the Saturday after Christmas."

"I'll be there." She hesitated a beat before asking, "Will you?"

"Yes, but not riding. Working the stock."

"Not competing?"

He thought he detected a hint of optimism in her voice, and hated disappointing her. "This jackpot is for high school students. There's a statewide junior rodeo coming up in January. Clay wants to give the kids an opportunity to practice before then."

"High school students? They're so young."

"I was competing at that age."

"I know." Deep creases knitted her brow.

"We don't use the same rodeo stock for them. The bulls and horses tend to be smaller. And Clay will require every participant to wear safety equipment or they don't compete."

He could see the topic distressed her. Too late, he remembered that Justin had been a senior in high school when he'd had his accident.

Fortunately, they reached Gavin's truck, and the discussion came to an end. Digging the keys from his pocket, he unlocked the door and retrieved the box of supplies.

"I'll carry it for you," he said when she held out her hands.

"Wait."

"Just this once, Caitlin, let me carry something for you without giving me a hard time."

"I don't care about the supplies." She hesitated, did that lower-lip biting thing that signaled she was nervous. "I'd planned on giving you this later tonight." She lowered the tote from her shoulder. "Now might be better, so you can put it in the truck."

His curiosity was piqued. "What is it?"

She removed a wrapped present from the tote bag and held it out to him. "Merry Christmas, Ethan."

He was floored. She'd gotten him a present, too.

Setting the supplies on the hood of the truck, he took the slim, rectangular package from her. "Thank you."

"It's nothing special... I hope you like it."

He tugged at the tape holding the colorful wrapping paper. "I'm sure I will."

The corner of a wooden picture frame peeked out. A moment later, he held a framed photograph in his hands, emotions rioting inside him.

"I noticed you don't have any pictures on the walls in your apartment yet," Caitlin explained. "I thought maybe this could be your first one."

"This is great." He smiled at her and tilted the picture for a closer look in the fading daylight. "I really like it." He also liked the effort she'd gone to and the thoughtfulness behind the gift.

"I hoped you would."

The photo was of him breaking Prince. It was one Justin had taken with his phone, now enlarged to an eight-by-ten. The angle was perfect. Both Ethan and Prince wore determined expressions, Ethan's goal to stay seated and Prince's to throw his rider. At the moment the photo was snapped, no clear victor was evident.

He rewrapped the picture and placed it on the floor in front of the passenger seat.

"Don't take this wrong, but I'm kind of surprised."

"Why?"

"You don't much like me bronc riding and breaking horses."

"Yes." Caitlin tipped her head appealingly to one side. "But it's your life and what you choose to do. I respect that and admire it, too. You've always been true to yourself, Ethan."

That wasn't quite accurate. If he was really true to himself, he'd haul Caitlin into his arms and kiss the socks off her.

"Be careful. I might start thinking you're not as tough as you claim."

"Maybe I'm not."

He was tempted to jump to all sorts of conclusions, and warned himself not to read too much into what she said. Becoming more tolerant of his chosen profession wasn't an open invitation back into her life.

"I have something for you, too." He reached inside his jacket pocket and removed his gift for her.

"Oh." Her eyes lit up. She accepted the present and, unlike him, tore at the paper with careless abandon. "Haverson's?" she asked, reading the name stenciled in gold.

"You've heard of them?"

"Yes." She cradled the box in her hands. "Before I open this, I'm going to say you shouldn't have. Everything in that store costs a small fortune."

Ethan chuckled. "One of the owners is a client of mine. He gave me a discount."

Nestled inside the tissue paper was a handmade Christmas tree ornament. Caitlin lifted it by the silk string and held it up. The wagon, a miniature replica of the one Ethan drove, spun in a circle, the glow from the parking-lot lights glinting off its shiny green paint.

"Ethan," she breathed. "It's charming."

"I know you said you weren't decorating this year because you hadn't decided whether to stay in Mustang Valley or not. I thought you should have something. Blame Sage and the girls. They've corrupted me with their Christmas spirit and—"

Caitlin didn't let him finish. Clutching the front of his jacket, she pulled him to her for a kiss. "I love it," she said, and pressed her lips to his.

Ethan was very glad he'd stowed away the picture she'd given him. Having two free arms enabled him to slip his hands inside her unbuttoned coat and draw her fully against him.

In the span of an instant the kiss went from sweet to sensual to searing. The moment his tongue touched her lips they parted for him. He took full advantage, and she encouraged him, unlike the night they'd kissed at the rodeo arena and he'd held back.

She tasted exactly as he remembered. Her body, firm yet yielding, molded to his. She teased and tortured him by sifting her fingers through the hair at the base of his neck and rocking ever so slightly.

Her soft moan was answered by a low groan from him.

The need to touch her became overwhelming. Too many clothes hampered his efforts, causing him great frustration. He settled for taking hold of her hips and aligning them with his.

"Caitlin?" Sage's call carried from the park.

Ethan cursed his future sister-in-law's lousy timing.

He broke off the kiss, gulping air to fill his deprived lungs. He tried to talk. All that came out was Caitlin's name and a ragged breath.

She sighed contentedly, smiled coyly. Standing on tiptoes she captured his lower lip between her teeth and tugged. It was something she used to do when they were younger, and it always drove him crazy.

Nothing had changed. His body jerked reflexively in response.

He kissed her again, hard, deeply, then pulled away while he still could. "I want to see you. Tonight. After the wagon rides."

"All right."

No objections? No arguments? No insisting he listen to reason?

"I'll get Gavin and Dad to take the wagon and horses home."

Caitlin leaned forward and rested her forehead on his chest. In a quiet voice she said, "We can go to my place."

"You sure?" Ethan lifted her face to his, not wanting there to be any misunderstanding between them.

"I'm sure." She retreated a step, and his hands fell away.

She'd made her decision about them and about tonight. Ethan didn't quite know what that decision was. He could only guess...and hope.

"THANK YOU, SIR." Caitlin put the donation for the mustang sanctuary in the jar. "The last ride will be leaving in about twenty minutes. The line starts over there."

They'd been busier tonight than last night, for which she was glad. The constant stream of customers over the past three hours had enabled her to avoid thinking of Ethan and what might occur later.

She'd invited him to her condo! That hadn't been her original intention. After they'd kissed, her mind shut down and her heart had come up with the idea. She could rescind the invitation, concoct some excuse. Only she didn't want to.

The ornament—Ethan must have had it custom-made for her—wasn't the only reason for the sudden change. He cared for her and showed her as much with his kindness to her brother and his respect for her feelings even when he didn't agree with them.

Hearing jingle bells, she turned her head. From this distance, the wagon looked like a wind-up toy. No, like the ornament. The illusion faded as the wagon drew nearer. Ethan sat in the driver's seat, the collar of his sheepskin jacket pulled up to protect his neck from the cold wind that sailed through the valley, his hat settled low on his brow.

Soon they would be leaving for her place. Her insides tingled with anticipation.

It was then she noticed the teenager sitting next to him was holding the reins, not Ethan. She heard him instruct the boy, "When we get to that tree, pull back and tell 'em 'whoa!'"

The wagon rattled to a stop a minute later, and the passengers, all in high spirits, piled out. Those waiting in line for the last ride of the night eagerly took their places.

Karen Lawler, the chair of the festival committee, stepped into her line of vision.

"Caitlin, my dear, the wagon rides have been an incredible success. Did you see the picture in today's newspaper?"

"No, but I heard about it."

"You should get a copy." The reindeer antlers Karen wore on her head tipped back and forth as she gestured excitedly.

"I'll check my computer in the morning. See if the picture's in their online edition."

"Do you think the Powells will be willing to give wagon rides again next year?"

"I have no idea. You can always ask."

"I was counting on you to do that, seeing as you're so close to them." There was no mistaking Karen's implication. Like half of Mustang Valley, she'd concluded Caitlin and Ethan were romantically involved.

Caitlin waited for a flood of embarrassment to heat her cheeks and tie her tongue. It didn't happen.

Interesting.

"I'm also counting on you to volunteer again," Karen continued.

A few weeks ago, Caitlin might have hesitated or declined, unsure if she was remaining in Mustang Valley or not.

"Of course I'll volunteer."

"Lovely," Karen trilled, and clasped Caitlin to her. "Merry Christmas, my dear. I must run. I'm meeting up with my grandchildren."

All the passengers had loaded up, and the wagon was ready to depart on its last run of the festival. Caitlin started clearing the table.

"You don't have to do that," Sage admonished, hurrying toward her. "Let me. You were only supposed to relieve me, and you ran the table the entire evening."

"You and the girls were enjoying the festival."

"Go get yourself an ice cream or a cup of coffee before all the vendors close for the night," Sage suggested.

"Okay. If you're sure you don't need me."

Caitlin didn't get ten feet away before discovering she really wasn't interested in food. If no one claimed the seat beside Ethan, maybe she'd go on the last ride with him.

The thought was barely formed when Cassie plunked down beside him and Gavin went over to talk to him.

Well, it had been a good idea while it lasted.

A minute later, the wagon still hadn't pulled out, and the passengers were getting restless. While Caitlin watched, the brothers traded places, with Gavin taking over the reins. He settled next to Cassie, while Ethan climbed carefully down, landing stiffly on the ground.

His leg must be bothering him. Or he was sore. Probably both.

She walked over to him. "Is something the matter?"

He smiled, a not-at-all-tired smile. "Gavin's taking the last ride for me, and then he'll drive the wagon home."

"Did you tell him about our plans?"

"Not a word. He's just giving me a break. It's been a long two nights."

The wagon pulled out at last to a chorus of cheers from its passengers.

"Do you mind if we take your van?" Ethan asked. "Dad's going to follow Gavin home in the truck."

"Of course not."

It wasn't until they were leaving the parking lot that Caitlin realized Ethan had no way home from her condo unless she drove him.

Chapter Thirteen

"You haven't been here before?" Caitlin asked.

"Actually, no."

Ethan didn't intend to gawk at his surroundings, but he couldn't stop himself. They stood at her front door while she fitted the key in the lock. He was quite certain the dirt road that used to cut through the center of Mustang Valley, the one he, Gavin, their father and the ranch hands had driven on a weekly basis, had been right where he was standing.

A surreal feeling came over him, as if he'd walked into someone else's dream.

"Everything's changed. So much."

"Must be hard on you." She twisted the knob and pushed open the door.

"Not as much as when I first came home. I haven't spent much time in Mustang Village." Hardly any until meeting Caitlin again.

They stepped inside her condo, and he was suddenly struck with a case of cold feet.

He was here at her invitation, which told him she was ready for more. But how much more? He'd hate to jump to the wrong conclusion.

She flipped a switch, and an overhead lighting fixture illuminated the empty entryway. To their right was a staircase.

Directly in front of them, a hallway. To their left, an open archway led to the living room.

"Public rooms downstairs. Bedrooms and bathroom upstairs." She laughed. "Though calling the second bedroom a 'room' is a stretch. I've seen bigger closets."

"This is nice."

Caitlin removed her jacket and held an arm out for Ethan's. He gave it to her. "It would be nicer with more furniture."

"Would you rather have a house?"

"Sure, eventually. For right now, this suits me. I don't have the time to take care of a yard or keep up on the maintenance a house would require."

She hung her jacket in the hall closet and draped Ethan's across the banister.

Was she planning on him making a fast exit?

"What about you?" she asked. "Ever think of living anywhere other than the ranch?"

"The bunkhouse is fine for now. Kind of cramped if I were…"

"Married with kids?" she finished for him.

"Something like that."

"You're really good with Cassie and Isa."

"Their parents might disagree. They've learned a few words from me that aren't, shall we say, appropriate for young ladies."

He followed Caitlin into the living room, which reminded him a little of his bunkhouse. The minimal necessities were there, a couch, a chair, a side table. What was missing were the decorative touches that turned a place into a comfortable home.

They were quite the pair, the two of them, moving through life, staying in different places but never putting down roots. What were they running away from?

What were they running to?

"I didn't even consider having kids for a long time." He sat on one end of the couch. "Not while I was in the marines."

"That's understandable."

Caitlin had brought the wagon ornament inside with her. She removed it from the box and placed it on the table beside an old lamp Ethan was sure had come from her parents' house. The ornament looked out of place sitting there all alone. Had he been wrong to get it for her? Maybe she wasn't ready to stay in one place.

Stay here with him.

"What about you? Want kids?"

"Two for sure. Maybe three," she added with a shy smile.

They'd never discussed having children, that Ethan could remember. In fact, they'd rarely discussed anything of a profoundly personal nature. Having fun had been their priority. Perhaps that was why when his mother died he hadn't turned to Caitlin and confided in her.

"Can I get you something?" she asked, a little too brightly. "Coffee? Beer? Eggnog?"

"Eggnog? I haven't had that for a long time. My mom used to make it."

"I'm afraid the kind I have comes in a carton from the grocery store. I can add a splash of brandy to it if you'd like." A mischievous glint sparked in her eyes.

He hadn't seen that glint since before he'd left for the marines. These days, she was always so serious.

"I'd like to, but you have to drive me home."

"That won't be for a while."

Oh, boy.

She went to the kitchen. Ethan waited on her couch, his heart chugging like a piston. It was just a cup of eggnog, he told himself. Nothing else.

But there had been that glint in her eyes....

She returned shortly and handed him a glass of frothy, creamy eggnog filled to the brim. Sitting on the other end of the couch, she kicked off her shoes, tucked her legs beneath her and sipped at her glass.

Her relaxed pose did nothing to slow the piston inside his chest.

He tasted his eggnog. "Not bad."

They talked after that, about nothing and everything. Gavin and Sage's wedding plans, old friends—who'd moved where and done what—and some of the more memorable shenanigans they'd pulled as teenagers.

More than once Caitlin's eyes misted with sentimental tears. They'd shared so much when they were younger. Ethan couldn't believe he'd walked away from it. From her.

After a particularly good laugh, she stretched out her legs on the couch. Her feet, in colorful Christmas socks, were inches from him.

What would she do if he pulled her feet into his lap?

"Another one?" Caitlin held up her empty glass.

"No, thanks." The eggnog hadn't been particularly strong, but it was probably better that they refrain from having more. "I should be getting home."

The talking had been enjoyable. A good beginning to wherever it was they were heading. Given the choice, he'd move a whole lot faster, but Caitlin was setting the pace, and he was very willing to let her.

"So soon?" She arched a foot toward him.

It was a very small movement, one that could easily be misread. He did nothing at first, then she arched it again. This time her toes brushed his thigh, light as a butterfly's wing.

What the hell.

He rested his hand on her ankle. When she didn't jerk

it away, he began kneading her foot, something he'd been aching to do since she'd shed her shoes.

She tipped her head back and closed her eyes. "Mmm… that feels good."

He couldn't take his eyes off her. The smooth expanse of her bare neck cried out for his kisses. Her slightly mussed hair curled sexily around her pink-tinged cheeks.

His hand moved from her foot to her calf. She made a contented sound as he continued massaging her with firm strokes.

In another minute, he wouldn't be responsible for his actions.

"I really need to go. Or not." He'd leave the choice to her.

Caitlin opened her eyes and sat up. Slowly pulling her legs away from him, she set her feet on the floor.

Disappointment cut through him.

Perhaps next time there would be a different ending to the evening.

He braced his hand on the armrest and started to stand.

She slid across the middle cushion separating them. "Or not," she stated.

Ethan sat back down and studied her face, searching for any sign of indecision or distrust. There was none. "Do you know what you're saying?" Honor dictated he give her one last opportunity to change her mind.

She linked her arms around his neck, snuggled against him and whispered, "Stay."

One word, and a whole world of possibilities opened up.

CAITLIN MIGHT HAVE QUESTIONED her actions right up until the moment she and Ethan kissed. They weren't just going to hit rough patches along the way, they were starting out in the middle of a big one.

But being intimate with him felt right and always had. She

loved hearing her name on his lips, repeated over and over between heated kisses.

His hand, large and strong and warm, slid down her back and under the hem of her shirt to caress bare skin. Her breasts flattened against his broad chest as she wriggled closer...closer...closer. His low exhalation of breath deepened into a groan as he tore his mouth away, to trail more kisses along the column of her neck.

She'd all but forgotten.

How could she?

Her fingers sought the buttons of his shirt, toyed with them, finally succeeded in unfastening the top three. A T-shirt impeded her quest for skin-to-skin contact, and she swore impatiently.

Ethan shifted beneath her, almost upending her. In one swift, deliberate move he stripped off his shirt and T-shirt, tugging them over his head and tossing them aside.

"Yes." She skimmed her palms along his hard muscles, felt them constrict as he sucked in air though his teeth. When she would have explored further, seen what other reactions she could arouse in him, he clasped both her hands between his and held them over his heart.

"This is no one-night stand. If it is for you, we stop now."

"No one-night stand." She sealed the promise with a kiss that instantly turned explosive.

The hair-trigger passion they ignited in each other was the same as when they were younger. It was also different. There was a hardness in Ethan she hadn't seen before, an intensity that was almost unbearable at times.

She imagined he noticed changes in her, too. The adventurous teenager had all but disappeared, replaced by an overly cautious woman afraid to take risks.

Except when it came to sex.

Then, and now, Caitlin had no qualms letting Ethan know

what she wanted, with actions and quietly murmured demands.

Suddenly, he broke off the kiss and set her away from him. "What?"

"Not here." He caressed her cheek with his fingertips. "Upstairs."

She rose from the couch, her body weightless like a bird taking flight, and extended her hand. Ethan took it. She turned, but before she could slip away, he wrapped his arms around her waist and pulled her to him, fitting her back to his front. His erection pressed into her as his lips nibbled the sensitive flesh where her neck joined her shoulder.

"So long," she murmured. "We waited so long."

He groaned in agreement.

She craved more but was loath to leave the warmth of his arms. Her burning need won out, and she led him to the stairs. As they climbed single file, she sensed his gaze on her and purposefully didn't hurry, even when they reached her bedroom. Inside the door sat a dresser with a small lamp. She turned it on. Light bathed the room in a warm yellow glow.

Ethan went to the bed and sat on the edge of the mattress. When she went to sit beside him, he tugged her between his open legs. Resting his hands on her waist, he laid his head on her chest.

"There's been no one for a long time." She couldn't explain her need to reveal such personal information.

"For me, either."

She brushed a fallen lock of black hair from his face. Leaning down, she kissed him again, holding his face in her palms as she ran her lips over his. He sat very still, hardly breathing.

"Touch me," she whispered.

He covered her breasts with his hands, squeezing them through the sweater she wore.

Waves of pleasure cascaded over her, and she tugged frantically at her clothes.

"Let me," he insisted, his voice a husky growl.

Who was she to object? She lifted her arms so he could remove her sweater. Her bra came next.

Filling his hands with her breasts, he ran his thumbs over her nipples until they hardened to tight peaks. It wasn't enough. At her urging, he leaned forward and drew one nipple into his mouth, then the other.

Her eyes drifted shut; her knees buckled slightly.

"Sweet. So sweet," Ethan murmured.

His mouth didn't stop there. It moved to other erogenous zones. The ridge of her collarbone. The valley between her breasts. Her navel.

She was wearing way too many clothes, Caitlin thought, and reached for the clasp on her jeans.

"I have protection," he said.

"Good."

He sat forward, removed his wallet from his pants pocket. "I'm only carrying this because—"

"I don't care why." She stroked his jaw. "I'm just glad you have it."

"Me, too."

She shimmied out of her jeans and panties, liking that he watched her every move with hungry eyes. Naked at last, she stood in front of him.

"You're incredibly beautiful." His gaze traveled from her toes to her face.

"Your turn."

Pushing himself off the bed, he attacked his belt buckle. When the clasp and zipper on his jeans defeated him, she came to his aid. Hooking his thumbs in the waistband, he slid his pants down. This time there were no shirttails to cover him, and Caitlin very much liked what she saw.

He sat back down, extending his left leg.

She knelt in front of him and removed his right boot. Then she grabbed his prosthesis by the ankle.

"Caitlin, sweetheart."

"Let me. I don't want there to be any barriers between us."

After a long moment, he swallowed and nodded. Once he'd loosened the cuff, she pulled gently. The prosthesis came off, sliding out of his pant leg. Giving it only the briefest of glances, she set it on the floor near the dresser.

Ethan removed his jeans, and she rested her hands on his thighs. Tenderly, she ran her fingers over his stump which began a few inches below his knee. He flinched once before relaxing as her gentle caresses continued over skin that was rough and riddled with scars in some places, and surprisingly smooth in others.

Caitlin's throat closed, and she swallowed a sob. In her mind, she could see him lying in some Middle Eastern street, buried in a pile of rubble, broken and bleeding. "This must have hurt."

"It still does some days."

"I'm sorry."

He tucked a finger under her chin and raised her face to his. "Don't be. I'm one of the lucky ones."

She straightened and went into his arms. "You have no idea how glad I am for that."

Ethan pulled her onto the bed and laid her on her back. She didn't stop to think about what he could or couldn't manage when it came to lovemaking. She had every confidence he'd show her.

They spent long minutes reacquainting themselves with each other's bodies. Ethan was still ticklish on his neck. She still broke out in goose bumps when he sucked on her earlobe. She delighted in the reactions her tongue and touch evoked in him. He grinned whenever she sighed softly or shivered with unrestrained pleasure.

She was past ready when Ethan nudged her legs apart and began stroking her intimate places. Her breathing went ragged, then stilled as his mouth moved down her torso to the inside of her thighs.

"I've dreamed of this," he said, placing his mouth on her.

So had she. Often.

Within minutes, seconds maybe, she was arching off the bed and hovering on the brink of climax.

"I want you inside me."

He crawled up her body, his mouth following the same trail up as it had down.

"Hurry!" she urged.

One quick tear and he had the condom open. Levering himself over her, he said, "Look at me."

She did, and he thrust inside her.

A shattering climax seized her almost immediately. She became a piece of driftwood riding a wild, storm-churned sea. He followed soon after, clinging to her as if she alone was responsible for anchoring him to the bed.

Eventually, he loosened his grip. When he started to roll off her, she held him and pleaded, "Not yet."

"For as long as you want, baby doll."

Baby doll. That was the name he'd called her in high school.

Caitlin felt her throat close again. She wasn't usually this weepy, but it had been a long time since she'd let down her guard. A long time since she'd felt so cherished.

"What if I want you with me a really long time?"

"I can do that." He rubbed his cheek along hers.

"I'm serious, Ethan."

He lifted his head to peer at her, his expression filled with—did she dare think it?—love.

"Me, too."

They would talk, needed to talk. Eventually. But not tonight.

"What would your family say if you didn't come home till morning?"

He did roll off her then and lay beside her, his good leg draped over her. "Probably that I finally came to my senses. And that you lost yours."

She punched him lightly in the arm. "Not possible."

"I won't hurt you again, baby doll. I swear."

Caitlin believed he would try his best to keep that vow. She also wasn't naive. Things changed without warning. Shit hit the fan. Worlds fell apart. It had happened to her before and could again.

They needed to proceed cautiously. Lift the lid of this box that was their new relationship one corner at a time.

As Ethan's hands roamed her body once more, inducing tiny tremors in her, she forgot all about erring on the side of caution.

Pushing him onto his back, she straddled his middle, determined to drive every thought from his mind.

GETTING TO THE RANCH early wasn't a problem. Ethan and Caitlin hardly slept all night. When they did doze, it was wrapped in each other's arms. He could still feel her tucked against him, warm and giving. Could taste her lips and skin, smell the light, flowery fragrance of her hair.

He'd brought only one condom with him. That hadn't stopped them from enjoying each other. They'd been careful and innovative, and next time—there would be many, many more next times—Ethan would be better prepared.

"When do you have to be at the festival today?" he asked.

Stifling a yawn, she turned her van into the driveway leading to the ranch.

"Not till ten. I can probably show up at eleven and no one will notice. I just need to be there when we close at four."

"Go home and take a nap," he told her, squeezing her hand.

"I think I will. What about you?"

"We're usually busy on Sundays, but with the festival, I doubt we will be today. If the girls don't pester me to take them on a ride, I might squeeze in a little shut-eye, too."

Any hopes they had of not being caught were dashed the moment Caitlin pulled into the open area in front of the stables. Gavin and Sage, up for an early morning outing, were helping the girls onto their horses.

Sage, Isa and Cassie waved, with big, welcoming smiles on their shining faces. Gavin simply nodded.

"Looks like you caught a break," Caitlin said airily. "No trail ride duty today." She didn't appear the least bit embarrassed at being spotted sneaking Ethan home.

He decided he shouldn't be, either. What he and Caitlin did in the privacy of her condo wasn't anybody's business, though there would be questions, he was sure, from Sage. His future sister-in-law didn't ascribe to the same to-each-your-own philosophy his father and brother did.

Caitlin continued to the bunkhouse, driving slowly, and parked out front. Their goodbye kiss went on and on.

"Any plans tonight, for after the festival?" he asked, thinking he could never get enough of her lush, ripe mouth.

"Nothing definite. I was considering buying a tree."

He liked the idea. It rang of permanence.

"Why don't I pick you up at four-thirty? We can go for an early dinner and then head to the tree lot."

"A date?"

"Yeah, a date."

"Mexican?"

"Wherever. You pick the place."

She paused for so long he thought she was going to say no. "Mexican it is."

"Good." *Very* good.

"We can talk."

"Ah." He'd been expecting that. "I suppose we have to."

"Yes, we do."

"I wish I could tell you I'll stop riding broncs."

"I wish I could tell you I have no problem with that." She lifted his hand and pressed the knuckles to her cheek. "Be patient with me. I swear I'll try my hardest to cope."

"I don't want you to always be worrying about me."

"It comes with the territory. Because of who I am, my profession, my brother, and because of how I feel about you."

He was tempted to ask her exactly how she felt about him but decided to wait until dinner tonight.

"One day at a time, okay?" she said.

"Sounds good to me."

"See you at four-thirty."

"If not sooner."

Her eyebrows rose.

"I was so busy with the wagon rides, I never got a chance to check out the festival. Is it possible to get a tour?"

"I'll see what I can arrange." Her mouth curved up in a smile that proved irresistible.

They were going to be all right, Ethan thought during another lingering goodbye kiss. This time, their relationship would last. It wouldn't be easy, but unlike when they were young, they knew full well the obstacles facing them, and that would make all the difference.

Chapter Fourteen

Caitlin could hardly believe it was Christmas Day already. The ten days following the Holly Days Festival had flown by in a blur. A happy, exciting, cloud nine kind of blur where she and Ethan were together every possible minute. They didn't run out of things to talk about or places to go. Neither did they tire of making love. Most nights they ended up at her place—no prying eyes and nosy family members, particularly those age twelve and under.

Missing the lower half of his left leg affected Ethan very little. He was an incredible lover. Attentive, considerate and generous. He also brought an emotional intensity to their lovemaking that hadn't been there years ago. She found that aspect more exciting than anything else.

She had wanted to spend today at the ranch with the Powells, but that wasn't possible because of her family obligations. No way on earth would her mother have tolerated her missing Christmas dinner.

By late afternoon, Caitlin couldn't wait a moment longer to see him, and after calling Ethan, left for the ranch with a promise to return to her parents' by seven. Or seven-thirty. Maybe even eight.

"You made it." He hurried across the back patio to meet her.

"Finally!" Eight o'clock for sure.

Caitlin had attended Christmas Eve service with the Powells, their first time stepping inside a church together since Ethan's mother's funeral. It had been a sentimental and moving experience, for Caitlin, as well.

Afterward, they'd returned to the ranch for coffee and dessert. Isa had hot chocolate. Cassie insisted on drinking coffee like the grown-ups. Her face as she forced down each sip had had everyone in stitches.

"I've missed you." Ethan lifted Caitlin off her feet and held her tight.

"Me, too." She liked being eye level with him, and showed him how much by giving him a smacking kiss on the lips.

He set her down then, but was slow to release her. "Hungry?"

"Are you kidding? Mom made enough food to feed five families."

"Same here. We'll be eating leftovers for a month."

"Everyone inside?"

"Mostly outside. Gavin wants to try riding Prince again today."

"Is he still giving Gavin a hard time?"

"It's funny. Gavin and Prince have always had this special connection. But for some reason, Prince doesn't like him riding him. He hasn't been able to get on the mustang since the day we broke him."

They strolled in the direction of the stables. Caitlin could see Gavin in the round pen with Prince.

"It's Christmas," she said. "Don't you guys ever take a day off work?"

"Riding Prince isn't work."

"Spoken like a true cowboy."

The setting sun gave everyone and everything it fell on long, skinny shadows, and a strong breeze from the east tousled hair and jackets. After the hectic family celebration, Caitlin welcomed the quiet change of pace the ranch afforded.

And she'd missed Ethan.

They hadn't resolved any of their issues. He was still riding broncs at Clay's arena. They didn't talk about it, and Caitlin chose not to think about it. Avoidance, yes. Denial, absolutely. And the day would come when they'd have to deal with both his lifestyle choices and her fears.

Next week, maybe, after New Year's and the high school jackpot. She wasn't about to put a damper on the holidays. Till then, she could almost pretend Ethan didn't court danger on a regular basis. It was easy as long as he didn't show up in her clinic injured, and she didn't have to watch him ride broncs at the rodeo arena.

"Merry Christmas," Caitlin said to Gavin when they reached the pen.

"Same to you," he answered distractedly, without taking his eyes off Prince.

At the sight of Ethan, the horse nickered and bobbed his head.

"He likes me better," he whispered to Caitlin.

"Who could blame him?" she whispered back.

He leaned over and gave her a peck on the cheek, which turned into a brief kiss, then a deep one.

"Ew!"

The comment came from Isa, who rode up on old Chico, the horse's dull clip-clop an excuse for a trot. Cassie was noticeably absent. She'd gone to visit her mother back in Connecticut during the school break between Christmas and New Year's.

"No comments from the peanut gallery," Ethan admonished the little girl, though his voice was hardly stern.

"Caitlin, see my new boots?" Isa stuck out her foot to show off a brand-new pink boot with black trim.

"Very pretty." It had taken some coaxing to get both girls to call her Caitlin away from school and the clinic. "How's Cassie doing?"

"She's coming home next week!" Isa squirmed excitedly. "I can't wait. Mama's going to take us to buy dresses for the wedding."

"Really?" Caitlin looked at Ethan for confirmation. "She's coming home?"

Gavin's custody arrangement with his daughter had been only temporary. There was a chance when he'd put her on the plane to Connecticut that she might not come back until the following summer, if then.

"Cassie called this morning to tell Gavin the news," Ethan said. "She asked to live with him permanently, and her mother agreed."

Caitlin's heart soared. What a truly wonderful Christmas present for the Powells. "I'm so glad for both of them."

"Gavin's happy. Or he was," Ethan corrected, "until today." He stooped and climbed through the rungs into the pen.

Caitlin watched, leaning her forearms on the second rung. Isa also watched, from her vantage point atop Chico.

Prince was in a mood, for sure. He alternately pawed the ground impatiently and swung his head from side to side. Twice he bared his teeth at Gavin.

Ethan approached the horse with less caution than Caitlin deemed prudent. She bit her tongue to stop from crying out.

"Easy, boy," he crooned.

To her surprise, Prince settled almost immediately. Even pushed his nose into Ethan's hand.

"Try getting on now," he suggested to his brother.

Gavin collected the reins, took hold of the saddle horn and raised his foot to put it in the stirrup.

Huffing loudly and humping his back, Prince danced sideways. He got only as far as Gavin's hold on him allowed.

"Stand!" Gavin commanded.

Prince stared at him, challenge burning in his eyes.

"What's with him?" Caitlin muttered.

"There's some new mares in the motel," Isa answered. "He always acts stupid around mares."

Caitlin didn't want to think about how knowledgeable Isa was on horse breeding.

Ethan reached out to stroke Prince's neck. The stallion permitted it, though he stood stiff and tense.

"That's it…" Ethan murmured.

Caitlin studied the two brothers, alike and yet so different. Both were intense. Ethan, however, was outgoing and gregarious, whereas Gavin tended to be reserved and private. Both loved passionately and both had suffered immeasurably when they'd lost a loved one. While Gavin withdrew, Ethan ran.

What would happen if Ethan was confronted with another devastating loss? Caitlin couldn't bear it if he left again.

"Go on, you ride him." Gavin nodded at Ethan. "One of us ought to."

"I'll warm him up for you."

With the ease of an experienced horse trainer, Ethan swung up into the saddle. Prince's legs trembled violently. But when Gavin released his hold on the bridle, the mustang circled the pen, responding perfectly to Ethan's cues. Walk, trot, lope and walk once more.

Man and horse were so beautiful. Ethan, tall and rugged in the saddle. Prince, strong and athletic, his long black mane and tail flowing in the wind like silky banners.

Caitlin wasn't the only one captivated. She glanced at Gavin and Isa and noted the two of them couldn't stop staring, either.

Ethan nudged Prince into a fast lope, then reined him to a

sudden stop that ended with a shower of dirt exploding from beneath his hooves.

Caitlin let out a small gasp.

"Back, boy, back."

Prince lowered his hind quarters and dug his hooves into the ground, each backward step given reluctantly—a hard-won victory for Ethan. Such strength and power in the horse, yet Ethan controlled it with ease. Thrived on it. Reveled in it.

It must be like that when he rode broncs.

Who was Caitlin to take that from him for purely selfish reasons?

After a half-dozen more turns around the pen at a comfortable trot, Ethan brought Prince to a halt beside his brother, an elated grin on his face.

"Your turn."

"What do you think?" Gavin asked the horse.

Prince rubbed his head on Gavin's jacket sleeve and exhaled lustily.

"All right, partner, if you say so." He patted the horse and took hold of the bridle so Ethan could dismount. "Let's give it a go."

Ethan grabbed the saddle horn and removed his left foot from the stirrup. Prince stood quietly, and Caitlin dared to relax. She could do this, she thought—watch Ethan ride and not suffer a panic attack.

One second the air was still, the next a cold gust of wind whipped past them. An empty plastic bag tumbled through the rails and into the round pen.

Prince balked and snorted, disliking the object and the crackling noises it made. That might have been the end of it if the plastic sack hadn't brushed against his underside. The horse went into a frenzy, kicking out with his back legs.

"What's wrong?" Isa asked in a small, scared voice.

Before Caitlin or anyone could answer her, Prince bolted, galloping around the pen. Ethan held on, his prosthesis flapping uselessly.

"Whoa, whoa!" he hollered, sawing on the reins.

Prince came to a stop, only to rear, his front legs slashing the air. Gavin dodged out of the way, escaping one sharp hoof that came perilously close to his face.

Ethan leaned forward in the saddle, struggling to maintain his balance.

Caitlin pressed her hands to her mouth, willing him to stay seated. He'd ridden a crazed Prince once before, on the day he broke him. He could do it again.

At last Prince came down. Nostrils flaring and flanks heaving, he stood quietly, even hanging his head.

"Is it over?" Isa squeaked.

Caitlin dared to breathe. "I think so."

"Easy there," Ethan murmured, and visibly relaxed.

Without warning, Prince tensed, then bucked again. High.

Ethan flew out of the saddle. Sailing head over heels, he landed in the dirt with a gut-wrenching thud, then lay immobile.

"Uncle Ethan!" Isa screamed.

Blood-chilling fear galvanized Caitlin, and she ran to the gate.

"Stay back!" Gavin shouted.

At the sound of his voice, Prince spun and charged, flinging Gavin against the railing.

Rearing yet again, the horse came down on Ethan's still form, his front hooves striking him repeatedly in the center of his back.

Free at last of both humans and the terrifying plastic sack, Prince loped in circles, stirrups bouncing and reins dangling.

"Are you all right?" Caitlin hollered to both men.

Neither one answered.

Disregarding her own safety, she flung the gate open. "Look out!"

At Gavin's warning, Caitlin dived to her left, narrowly avoiding being trampled by Prince as he lunged through the opening and thundered toward the stables.

Caitlin raced into the round pen. "Ethan, can you hear me? Ethan!" She dropped down beside him, frantically taking in every detail. The closed eyes. The irregular breathing. The cuts and contusions. "Ethan, sweetie, can you hear me?"

His eyelids fluttered once, then went still.

Gavin stumbled toward them.

She looked up at him. "Do you have a cell phone on you? Call 911."

"Give him a minute. He'll come around."

"A minute? Are you insane?"

She was normally levelheaded in a crisis, one of the qualities that made her a good nurse. With Ethan hurt, being levelheaded flew out the window.

"Call 911 and do it now!"

Removing his phone from his pocket, Gavin placed the call.

Caitlin touched Ethan's bare head, his arm and back with just the tips of her fingers. She didn't dare disturb him, having no idea the seriousness of his injuries. A concussion, no doubt. Fractured bones. Internal injuries. A broken neck. Oh, dear God, he'd landed so hard, and his left arm lay at an unnatural angle. His hat sat upside down on the other side of the pen.

"Ethan, please." Tears blurred her vision, and her voice splintered. "Talk to me."

"He's going to be okay."

She was only dimly aware of Gavin's voice as it penetrated her escalating terror.

"You don't know that."

Her composure crumpled. She was once again in the hospital, pacing the halls, waiting for the doctors to deliver news of Justin's condition. And when it finally came, it had devastated her and her parents.

Sobbing, she barely felt Gavin's hand giving her shoulder a comforting squeeze.

"Go fetch your mother," he told Isa, who scampered off.

"Stay with me, sweetie…" Caitlin would give anything to hold Ethan in her arms, lay his head in her lap and stroke his hair. All she could do was watch helplessly as his chest rose and fell with each shallow breath he drew.

Where was the closest fire station? She couldn't remember.

Ethan groaned softly.

"I'm here. I'm here." She tentatively stroked his cheek with her index finger.

"See, I told you," Gavin said. "He'll be fine."

Only, Gavin was wrong. Ethan didn't rouse, and his face lost even more color.

"Gavin!" Sage came out of nowhere. "What can I do?"

"Keep everyone away. Direct the emergency vehicles here. And tell Javier to find Prince."

How could he care about that damn stupid horse after it had nearly killed his brother?

Finally, mercifully, she heard the distant wail of a siren.

"Help's on the way, sweetie," she told Ethan. "It won't be long now."

Long until what? The doctors came to the hospital waiting area and delivered a hopeless prognosis?

Ethan had been through so much already. He'd lost his mother and his leg. Plus the cattle operation that had been in his family for a hundred years. It wasn't fair. He didn't deserve tragedy heaped upon tragedy.

The paramedic unit pulled up alongside the round pen.

Two uniformed men rushed through the gate, lugging equipment. A fire truck came next. As Gavin guided Caitlin out of the way so the paramedics could examine Ethan, more uniformed men arrived. Seven altogether.

They asked questions Caitlin couldn't answer. When she pressed them for details on Ethan's condition, they gave noncommittal responses.

"I'm a nurse."

"Then you know to let us do our jobs," one of the men said, not unkindly.

Within minutes, they had Ethan hooked up to a heart monitor and an IV. They'd checked his respiration, taken his pulse and his blood pressure, and assessed his injuries. He came to, but only fleetingly, and wasn't coherent.

Understanding every move the paramedics made, every medical term they used, just made the situation worse for Caitlin. His vitals weren't good, and his failure to respond was of concern.

The ambulance arrived with its EMTs. Ethan's head and neck were immobilized, and he was carefully lifted onto a stretcher, then transported to the vehicle.

"Can I go with him?" Caitlin beseeched, her gaze going from Gavin to the EMTs.

"It would be better if you met us at the hospital."

The female EMT slammed the ambulance door shut, the sound echoing through the empty corridors of Caitlin's heart.

ANOTHER HOSPITAL, ANOTHER waiting room. Caitlin hadn't bitten her nails since she was in middle school, but her right thumbnail was now gnawed to the quick. She was starting on her left one when Justin wheeled into the waiting room.

She jumped up from her chair. Although she was glad to see him, his presence evoked memories of the terrible night she and her parents had spent after his fall from the cliffs.

"Any word?" he asked, throwing his arms wide.

She bent and held him for many seconds. "He regained consciousness in the ambulance. Was able to answer questions, like what's his name and what day it is."

"That's good."

"Yes, but he doesn't remember the accident."

"He may not."

True. Hadn't Ethan told her he still didn't remember the car bomb explosion?

"He's in surgery now."

"What for?"

"Six broken ribs, one close to his lungs. They also want to make sure there are no internal injuries."

The Powells sat huddled together on the couches where they had waited along with Caitlin for the last hour and a half—Gavin, his father, Sage and Isa. Their worried expressions told a silent story. Wayne Powell was a wreck. When he wasn't pacing he was staring out the window. Was he thinking of his late wife, just as Caitlin was thinking of her brother?

"You okay?" Justin asked.

"Fine."

"You sure? Your hands are shaking."

Were they? Caitlin glanced down, startled to see that her brother was right.

"It's nothing." She rubbed her palms on her pants.

"Mom and Dad said to call if you need anything."

Justin took her back to the Powells. They greeted him like one of the family, then everyone fell silent again.

Just when Caitlin was about to crawl out of her skin, the surgeon made an appearance and was instantly mobbed.

"How is he?" Ethan's father asked before anyone else could.

The doctor's eyes were somber, and she didn't mince

words. "He's in stable condition, but make no mistake, his injuries are serious. Had the horse landed differently, your son might not be here. He's a very lucky man."

Ethan had said almost the same thing about the explosion when he'd lost his leg. How often could a person escape death?

"What are his injuries?" Gavin asked.

"He sustained a concussion in the fall, and right and left rib fractures when the horse stepped on him—eight in total. One of the fractured ribs missed puncturing his lung by only a few millimeters. His spleen is bruised. Thankfully, it didn't rupture. We need to watch that closely over the next few weeks. And two herniated disks."

The surgeon went on to explain Ethan's treatment, expected hospital stay and rehabilitation.

"When can we see him?" Wayne Powell asked.

"As soon as he's been moved to a regular room. About a half hour to an hour. When you do see him, tell him I said to be more careful next time."

Once the surgeon left, everyone started talking, their relief needing an outlet. Sage broke into racking sobs.

Caitlin wanted to cry, too, but something prevented her. She kept remembering the surgeon's warning.

Had the horse landed differently, your son might not be here.... Tell him I said to be more careful next time....

Next time.

She should never have told him she would try to cope with his bronc riding and breaking horses. Never given him that photo.

Would he have stopped for her?

Maybe, maybe not. She'd basically given him her blanket approval.

This was her fault.

All right, maybe not all her fault. But partially her fault.

Like Justin's injury.

"You okay, sis?"

Caitlin blinked, shook her head to clear it. "Yeah. If you want to leave now, go ahead."

"I'll stay until after you've seen him."

"Thanks." She swallowed.

"Ethan's going to be fine."

"Until the next time."

Gavin turned to stare at her.

She hadn't meant to say that out loud.

Justin didn't seem to notice. "He's tough."

But was she? Caitlin had her doubts.

"You heading back to Mom and Dad's or going home?" he asked.

"Neither. Tamiko's family is having an open house tonight and they invited me. I thought I might drop by for an hour after I leave here."

"What about her boyfriend?"

"He'll be there, too. Unfortunately."

"Oh, Justin."

"Quit worrying about me, sis."

"I can't. I won't. You're my brother." She'd almost said *baby* brother. He wouldn't have liked that.

"Tamiko can do better than him. When she finally wises up, I want to be there, waiting in the wings."

"What if she doesn't wise up? I hate to see you get hurt."

"Life comes with risks."

"We can minimize them."

"We can also live in a bubble." He smiled at her. "What fun is that?"

Not long after, a nurse came by to inform the family that Ethan could receive visitors.

"Don't overwhelm him," she advised. "He's still pretty groggy and needs his rest."

"Isa and I will wait for you," Sage said.

"But I want to see Uncle Ethan," Isa pouted.

"We will, *mija*, tomorrow. You can draw him a picture." Isa was only slightly mollified.

"I can come back tomorrow, too," Caitlin said. Now that the moment to see Ethan had arrived, she was having reservations.

"No," Gavin said. "He'll be furious with us if we let you leave."

They took the elevator to the fourth floor. Outside Ethan's door, Caitlin hesitated. His brother and father went ahead of her. She watched from the doorway, her feet frozen to the floor.

She was a nurse and knew what every beep and readout on the monitors meant. He was stable; she could see that at a glance. His complexion was pasty, he barely moved and his responses were slow. But his injuries weren't life threatening, and according to the surgeon, he'd make a full recovery.

Except, at this moment, she wasn't a nurse who thought logically and dispassionately. She was scared and worried and guilty as hell. Seeing Ethan's prosthesis leaned up against the chest of drawers intensified her emotions.

He's a very lucky man.

She gave his brother and father time alone with Ethan. He was considerably more alert than she'd expected. Like Justin had said, Ethan was tough.

He asked about the fall, had Gavin repeat the story twice. He also wanted to know the details of his injuries and what procedure had been performed during the surgery. As they continued talking, he became more and more groggy. Between his injuries and the pain medication, it was to be expected.

"Did the doctor mention how soon until I can ride again?" he asked.

Ride again! How could he even be thinking of that?

"Six weeks at least," Gavin answered. "Depends on how fast you recover. Knowing you, it won't be long."

Gavin was encouraging him. What kind of brother was he? Had he not heard the doctor's warning?

"Maybe you should give it a while," Wayne Powell said, the only sane person in the room as far as Caitlin was concerned.

"Come on, Dad." Ethan smiled crookedly. "Didn't you teach us when we fall to get right back in the saddle?"

And that was exactly what Ethan had done when he'd lost his leg. Why would she think a concussion, a half-dozen broken ribs and a multitude of minor injuries would stop him?

She didn't stand a chance.

"Where's Caitlin?" he asked, slurring her name.

"She's here." Gavin turned and motioned her into the room.

One step was all she could manage before walking into an invisible wall.

"Hey," Ethan said, lifting his head. He peered at her with unfocused eyes, then fell back on the pillow. "Sorry, I'm a little dizzy."

Caitlin, too. Her own head swam and her stomach roiled.

"I'll come back later." She grabbed the doorjamb, desperately needing support. "When you feel better."

"No, don't leave," Ethan croaked.

The invisible wall wouldn't let her through.

"Come on, Dad." Gavin patted him on the back. "Let's give them a minute alone."

They squeezed past her into the hallway, leaving Caitlin alone with Ethan.

She mustered all her courage. For such a small room, it was a very long walk to the bed. She attempted to draw on her nursing experience, use it as a shield.

It didn't work. She wasn't in love with her patients.

"How are you?"

It should have been her asking him the question.

"Me? You're the one who got bucked off a horse." And nearly killed. She leaned down and kissed his forehead, a lump rising in her throat.

"I'm sorry," he said.

"For what?"

"Ruining your Christmas."

"You didn't," she said, because that was what he needed to hear. Inside, she was dismayed and distraught. The day had gone from one of the most joyous she'd spent to one of the worst. "I'm just glad you're going to be okay."

"What about us? Will we be okay?"

The lump in her throat burned.

She wanted to reassure him. Tell him that nothing had changed. They were as good as they'd always been. But the past two and a half hours had taken a terrible toll on her, and she had yet to assess the damage.

"Let's talk tomorrow."

"That sounds like a brush-off." He was fighting to stay awake.

She would not have this conversation in the hospital with him lying there in pain and doped up on medication.

"You need to rest," she said.

"That's Nurse Carmichael talking."

"Yes, and she knows best right now." Rest for him, space for her.

"It was an accident."

She hated that word. People used it when they didn't want to claim any responsibility for a bad decision they'd made.

"I'll see you in the morning."

"You're running away." The medications he was on didn't disguise the reproving tone of his voice.

Why was it okay for him to leave and not her?

His eyes drifted closed and the frown he'd been wearing vanished. Seconds later, he was sound asleep.

She had no trouble crying now. Tears streamed from her eyes as she staggered past the nurse's station to the elevator.

She was in the parking lot before it dawned on her she had no vehicle, having ridden over with the Powells. Were they still in the hospital? She didn't remember seeing them in her hasty exit. Or Justin. Maybe he could drop her off at the ranch to fetch her van, on the way to…where was it he was going? Tamiko's parents' open house.

Thinking was hard, more than Caitlin could deal with at the moment.

Tears continued to fall. Someone asked her if she was all right. Fortunately, sobbing people weren't uncommon at hospitals.

Caitlin found her way to a bench outside the entrance, sat and waited for her composure to return. It did, though her hold on it was fragile and, she feared, temporary.

With quaking hands, she located her cell phone and dialed Justin's number.

"What's wrong?" he asked upon hearing her voice.

He knew what she'd been through after his fall, and would understand her better than anyone else.

"I can't keep doing this," she blurted. "I just can't."

Chapter Fifteen

Ethan hobbled to the pasture behind the barn and the spe-
cially designed paddock. Prince greeted him with a friendly
whinny and a head toss.

"Don't try and get on my good side. It's too late for that."

He stroked the horse's head and sleek neck. They'd come
a long way since his capture, he and this once wild mustang
Had forged a lasting bond against all odds.

Ethan wished he could say the same for him and Caitlin

While he and Prince still had considerable work ahead of
them, they were well on their way. He understood the horse
accepted him for what he was, flaws and all. Tempered his
high hopes with reasonable expectations. Prince, Ethan was
convinced, felt the same about him.

He wished he had some idea—*any* idea—of how Caitlin
felt about him.

She hadn't returned even one of his phone calls in the six
days since she'd fled his hospital room. He still wasn't quite
sure what had happened. Damn concussion and pain pills
had messed with his memory.

What he did remember was that she'd left in tears. Based
on what his brother had witnessed in the waiting room, and
the previous disagreements Ethan had had with Caitlin, he
guessed his cowboy ways were the cause.

How were they supposed to resolve their differences if she didn't take his phone calls?

Justin was no help. He was busy job hunting now that he'd finished college. Ethan had talked to him once, and his advice was to be patient. Caitlin would come around.

Ethan had contemplated jumping in his truck and driving to her condo, surprising her with an unannounced visit, but he'd barely made it to the paddock without stopping four times to rest and let an excruciating spasm recede. Coughing hurt. Yawning, too. Sneezing nearly knocked him to his knees.

Dammit!

Ethan removed his hat and drove his fingers through his hair. He despised this helplessness. He was a doer, a fixer, a problem solver. And he was convinced he could fix whatever had gone wrong with him and Caitlin if he could just talk to her.

"Happy New Year, buddy." Clay came up beside him, his arm raised.

Ethan glared at his best friend. "You clap me on the back, and I swear, I'll deck you."

Clay chuckled. "And I'd deserve it." He gave Prince a lengthy appraisal. "You two make up yet?"

"I was never mad at him to begin with. He's a wild animal. Former one, anyway. I let my guard down when I shouldn't have." Ethan noticed Clay's clothes for the first time. "You going somewhere special?"

"Conner's party. Want to come along?"

Ethan had forgotten all about it. He and Caitlin had planned on going, before he got hurt. Even if he was up to it, which he wasn't, he wouldn't attend without her.

"Maybe next year."

"I noticed the clinic was open tonight. Guess they're having extended hours on account of the holiday."

"And your point?"

"Caitlin's van was in the parking lot." Clay leaned against the stall. "She's on duty and can't leave the clinic. If you were to, say, show up, she'd have no choice but to listen to you."

Ethan grinned. He'd always liked the way Clay thought. "I'd need a ride. I can't drive yet."

"Let's go."

Ethan spent a few minutes cleaning up before leaving with Clay. Caitlin's van was indeed parked in the clinic lot, just as his friend had said, and a handwritten sign on the door advertised extended hours.

"I don't know how long I'll be," he told Clay.

"I don't care, I'm not sticking around."

"You're not?"

"You'll have to find your own way home. I'm counting on Caitlin."

Ethan was, too.

Thanks to his busted ribs, the door to the clinic weighed about three times as much as it had before. Clenching his teeth, he pushed it open and stumbled inside, setting off the buzzer.

"Hi, can I help you?" a pleasant young woman at the counter asked. There was no one else in the waiting room.

"I'm here to see Caitlin Carmichael."

"She's on duty. Is this an emergency?"

He didn't hesitate. "Yes."

"Can I have your name?"

This time, he did hesitate. "Ethan Powell."

The woman picked up the phone and pressed a button. After a moment, she said, "There's an Ethan Powell here to see you. He says it's an emergency."

Seconds ticked by. So many he started having serious doubts.

Finally, the woman hung up the phone. "She'll be out in a minute. Have a seat."

Ethan didn't. Getting up again would be too strenuous. He waited by the window, which gave him an unobstructed view of the door to the exam rooms. The minute the receptionist had promised stretched into five, then eight, then—son of a bitch, what was taking her so long?

A young couple came into the clinic, the man looking like death warmed over and complaining of flu symptoms. While they filled out the paperwork, Ethan debated asking the receptionist to page Caitlin again.

Before he could make his way to the counter, she came through the door.

"Sorry I'm late. I was with a patient." Lines of tension etched her face, and dark circles surrounded her eyes. She hadn't been sleeping well.

"I thought you might be avoiding me."

She didn't acknowledge his joke. "Is everything okay? Are your injuries bothering you?"

"I'm fine."

"You said it was an emergency." She eyed him suspiciously.

"It is. We need to talk."

"I'm at work," she replied in a low, terse voice.

"Take a break."

Her lips thinned.

"Ten minutes. That's all I ask. I wouldn't be here if you'd answered any of my fifteen or twenty phone calls."

"Fine. Let me get my coat and tell Dr. Lovitt."

She returned a few minutes later, slipping her arms into her coat sleeves as she walked to the door.

He beat her there and opened it for her, paying the price as a spear of agonizing pain sliced through him.

"Honestly, Ethan," she snapped. "You don't always have to do things for me, especially when you're hurt."

"My father raised me to be a gentleman."

She squeezed her eyes shut. "I didn't mean to insult you."

"You didn't."

He gestured toward the tables and chairs in front of the coffee shop next door. Caitlin pulled her own chair out when he would have done it for her. She sat gracefully, Ethan with considerable effort.

"How are you doing?" she asked.

"I'll live."

His answer had been intended as another joke, but it was obvious by her sudden stiffening that he'd struck a chord. He hadn't had long to mentally compose what he wanted to say to her tonight, but talking to her had consumed his thoughts for days. He should've done a better job of breaking the ice.

"It was an accident. Not your fault, not my fault. Not even Prince's fault. The best-trained horses spook sometimes at nothing."

"I know that. I don't blame myself or Prince."

"But you blame me?"

She remained stubbornly silent. When she spoke at last, her words were measured.

"You are who you've always been. You like taking risks. Tempting fate. Pushing your limits. It's what made you a good soldier, good at training horses and a competitive athlete."

"And you don't like taking risks."

"No." Her eyes were full of misery and regret. "And I don't think I can be with someone who does."

A suffocating pressure closed around his chest, worse than when he'd broken his ribs. On some level he'd been expecting this.

"I'll quit riding broncs. Breaking horses, too."

"I wouldn't ask that of you. You were right when you said it isn't fair for one person to force another to give up something that's important to them."

"No, I was wrong." God, he was losing her. He could feel her ebbing away like the ocean at low tide. "People have to make compromises for a relationship to work."

"Giving up your dream isn't a compromise, and I refuse to be the cause of your unhappiness."

A sense of déjà vu came over Ethan, crushing him. He remembered a similar conversation from nine years ago that had gone much like this one. Except he'd been the one saying, "I refuse to be the cause of your unhappiness."

"The day you were hurt was a nightmare for me," she continued, a tremor in her voice. "The sight of you in that hospital bed—I couldn't deal with it. I nearly broke down. I did later, outside the hospital."

"Why? You're a nurse."

"Not that night I wasn't." She sniffed. "I should have come over to see you after you were released. But telling you when you were laid up…"

"Telling me what?" Ethan braced himself, instinctively knowing that whatever came next was going to change his life irrevocably. Again.

She sat up, determination in her expression. "I'm sorry, I can't see you anymore."

"You're part of me. The missing piece."

"One you can live without." She stood, her chair squeaking as it scraped across the concrete. "You have before."

She left him there, alone in the cold.

Sometime later, a few minutes or an hour, Ethan couldn't be sure, Clay appeared. Had he waited all this time?

"Come on, buddy. I'll take you home."

Ethan went with him, needing help finding the truck.

He thought he might be lost for the rest of his life.

CAITLIN SAT ON THE CLOSED toilet lid and stared at the double pink lines on the testing wand she held. Reality, which she'd successfully kept at bay since yesterday morning, hit her full force. The wand dropped to the floor as she caught her falling head in her hands. Home pregnancy tests weren't one hundred percent accurate. Which was why she'd taken a second one this morning. The chance that both tests showed a false positive was astronomical.

She was pregnant.

How had that happened?

Of course she knew how it happened, but...*how?* They'd used protection. Condoms weren't infallible, as she'd heard doctors tell patients many times. And there was that first night she and Ethan had spent together after the Holly Days Festival, when they'd had only one.

She mentally counted backward. Three, no, four weeks along.

What was she going to do? She pressed her fingertips to her throbbing temples and rubbed.

If she told Ethan, he'd go all Ethan on her. Want to get married. Raise the baby together. On top of all the other problems they had, they'd be adding having an instant family to the mix. Not the best way to start out.

She could leave Mustang Valley, maybe even Arizona. Go stay with her college friend in Columbus and have the baby there.

Then what? She couldn't come home, not if she didn't want Ethan to find out. And he would, eventually. Someone would see her and the baby and mention it.

No, she either told him outright and dealt with the consequences, or left Mustang Valley for good.

Not the kind of decisions a new mother should have to make. This was supposed to be a joyous moment she would treasure the rest of her life.

And, suddenly, it was.

She was pregnant! Going to have a baby! Elation bubbled up inside her, then spilled out in a giddy laugh. Tomorrow or next week was soon enough to decide what and if to tell Ethan. She was barely a month along, after all. For now, she would keep her condition a secret, bask in her happiness alone until the right moment to share it.

She no sooner emerged from the bathroom than her cell phone rang. A glance at the caller ID informed her it was Justin. Guilt needled her. She hadn't spoken to her brother much these past two and half weeks. Or her parents. She'd taken the breakup with Ethan hard. Loss of appetite. Insomnia. Churlishness. Depression. You name it, she had it.

After one look her parents would instantly know something was wrong. Caitlin wasn't up to fielding their questions. Justin would be worse. He'd pester her until she spilled her guts.

Briefly, she considered not answering his call, but another prick of guilt compelled her to press the receive button.

"Hey."

"Why didn't you tell me you and Ethan called it quits?"

"We weren't actually going together." A few weeks didn't constitute a relationship.

They were, however, long enough to create a life.

"I knew you were upset with him, but I figured you'd resolved it."

"How did you find out?" Caitlin asked.

"Ethan told me. He's really bummed."

"You saw him?"

"I'm here now. At the ranch."

"You are?" She wanted to ask how Ethan was doing. Instead, she voiced the second question on her mind. "What are you doing there?"

"Tamiko and I signed up for riding lessons."

"Riding lessons!" This conversation couldn't get any weirder. "Since when?"

"I thought you'd be here, considering it's Sunday afternoon, and I'd surprise you."

Wait a minute. Rewind. "Riding lessons? I thought you agreed that wasn't a good idea."

"I never said any such thing. You lectured and I listened."

"Look what happened to Ethan." Fear gripped her and shook her like a rag doll.

"I'm not riding bucking horses."

"I don't care if you're riding a pony. It's too dangerous."

"No more dangerous than white-water rafting on the Colorado River."

She'd been a wreck when he'd taken that harebrained trip last summer. "At least you were wearing a life jacket."

"And this time I'll be wearing a helmet."

She had to stop him. "I'll be right there."

"Don't come if you're planning on making a scene."

"When have I ever made a scene?" She grimaced. "Okay, I take that back. I have made a scene or two, but only because I care."

"See you when you get here," he said, and disconnected.

Caitlin didn't waste any time. She grabbed her purse and keys and hit the door at a run.

Turning into the Powells' driveway, she reduced her speed to the legal limit and was immediately ashamed of herself. She didn't usually drive like a maniac.

Upon reaching the open area in front of the stables, she started searching for Justin.

And, yes, Ethan.

She'd missed him. And this place. His family, too. How had they become so important to her after only a few weeks?

Maybe because they always were.

She scoured the main arena, where a dozen riders were exercising their horses, none of them Justin.

At last she spotted him in the round pen. The same pen where Ethan had been injured when riding Prince. Justin sat astride a horse, Ethan standing beside him. Tamiko straddled the fence, the empty wheelchair not far from her.

Where was her boyfriend?

Caitlin drove her van right up to the pen, hit the brakes and slammed the vehicle into Park. Shoving the door open, she bailed out, tripping over her own feet in her haste.

"Justin!"

"That didn't take long." An exuberant grin split his face.

"Are you okay?" She was aware of Ethan watching her, studying her.

Her body, always attuned to him, hummed in response.

"Great! This is amazing." Justin shielded his eyes from the afternoon sun and regarded the horizon. "I can't believe how far I can see. Look at the mountains."

The motion unbalanced him and he teetered in the saddle. Caitlin let out a yelp. "Ethan, help him!"

"Whoa!" Justin grabbed the saddle horn.

Ethan reached up and placed a steadying hand on Justin's leg. "Hang on."

He looked considerably better than the night he'd shown up at the clinic, but not strong enough to catch Justin if he fell. Someone else must have lifted her brother onto the horse. Someone else should be here now.

"No problem." Justin let go of the saddle horn.

Ethan started walking, leading the horse, which Caitlin now recognized as old Chico.

She was going to kill both Ethan and her brother.

"He's doing great, don't you think?" Tamiko said.

Caitlin looked around. "Where's...um..."

"Eric? I really don't know."

She didn't have time to process Tamiko's answer because Justin clucked to Chico, and the horse broke into a run.

All right, not a run. A very, very sedate trot.

Ethan walked beside the horse, letting the lead rope dangle. If Chico reared or bucked, there was no way he could restrain him. Justin would be hurt.

At least he was wearing a helmet and, she noticed upon closer inspection, a safety vest. If Ethan had been wearing a helmet and vest when he fell off Prince, he might not have broken his ribs or sustained a concussion.

Wait! Justin didn't have a harness. Ethan said at Thanksgiving that he had harnesses Justin could use. What if he slipped again?

"Be careful," Caitlin said, sounding like the broken record she was, her white-knuckled hands gripping the railing. Thank God there was no wind today. She scanned the immediate vicinity for stray plastic bags anyway.

"I can't wait for my turn." Tamiko glowed.

Caitlin, on the other hand, couldn't speak. Her heart had lodged in her throat.

Was she the only one terrified?

Yes, she was—the only one. Not Justin or their parents or Tamiko. Certainly not Ethan. And he should be more than anyone, after what had happened to him.

All right, she was a little overprotective. A lot overprotective. But she was hardly unreasonable.

Was she?

She looked at her brother, really looked at him. He was enjoying himself. Now that she thought about it, he always seemed to be enjoying himself. For the past several years, anyway. Ever since he took up wheelchair athletics.

He grinned confidently at Tamiko as he rode past her, a far cry from the insecure, self-conscious geek he'd been in high school.

Caitlin had to stop seeing him as disabled and start seeing him as what he was, a capable, competent young man with endless potential and no need of a hovering older sister.

"Yes, he's doing well," she said, sensing a shift inside her.

After a few more circuits, Ethan led Justin through the gate. They stopped in front of Caitlin and Tamiko.

"What do you think?" Justin preened. "Are we ready for the races?"

Tamiko's smile was radiant and for him alone. "You were awesome."

"I'm impressed," Caitlin admitted, her pride overflowing.

"You're not just saying that?"

"Definitely not."

"Any chance I can ride around the ranch?" he asked Ethan.

"Not by yourself. Not yet."

She sent Ethan a silent thank-you.

He nodded, and the yearning in his eyes reached into her, tugging at her heart and her belly, where she carried their child.

"Can Tamiko take me?"

"How about your sister? And just up and down in front of the stables."

"Me!" she squeaked. "What if Chico starts bucking? I can't hold on to him."

"He won't buck. He has the temperament of a kitten." Ethan thrust the lead rope into Caitlin's hands. "Go on. You can do it."

He was talking about more than her brother riding a horse, she was sure.

"It'll be okay, sis," Justin said, also talking about more than riding.

Yes, it would be okay.

The shift in her was suddenly complete and seamless.

Giving Ethan one last long glance, she took a step, then

another. Chico followed like the good, dependable horse he was.

As she and Justin passed the office, he said to her, "Thanks. I know this isn't easy for you."

She didn't respond, afraid she might start crying. Must be hormones.

"You have to stop feeling bad about the accident," Justin said. "I don't. Haven't for a long time."

"But you lost the use of your legs."

"Pretty incidental in the larger scheme of things."

"No, it isn't!"

"It is. I'm better off now than I ever was. I've got my degree. Have two job offers I'm considering. I play sports. White-water raft. I'm learning to ride a horse." He patted Chico's neck. "Have a girlfriend."

"Tamiko? What about Eric?"

"She dumped him. For me. For *me*," he repeated, wearing the goofy grin of a besotted man.

Caitlin wasn't just proud of him, she was impressed. "I'm glad." As long as he didn't get hurt.

She had to stop thinking like that—*would* stop thinking like that.

"I'm happy, sis."

He was. She could see it in his face, hear it in his voice.

The weight she'd been carrying for the last six years didn't lift entirely, but it decreased. Eventually, soon, she'd be free of it.

"You should be happy, too. Ethan loves you."

"I messed up with him." She sniffed and Chico gave her arm a sympathetic nudge.

"Nothing you can't repair."

"I don't know how."

"Talk to him. I guarantee, he'll listen."

"I'm not sure there's a point to it. I can't handle his bronc riding. You saw how I was at the hospital."

"You'd be surprised what you can handle if you have to. Look at me. Look at Mom and Dad."

He made a good argument. And she already felt stronger. Amazing what release from guilt could do for a person.

Chico turned abruptly and started walking in the opposite direction.

"Hey, there!" Caitlin pulled on the lead rope, then gave the horse his head. Chico was going exactly where she wanted to—back to Ethan.

He must have noticed a change in her because his whole countenance lit up at her approach.

"Can we go somewhere to talk?" she said when they were close enough.

His shoulders straightened as if he, too, had had a weight lifted from them. "I'll find Conner and T.J. so we can get Justin down."

"I'm fine," Justin said. "Tamiko will lead me around for a while."

Tamiko jumped off the fence in eager anticipation. Caitlin passed her the lead rope, and the pair took off.

By unspoken agreement, Caitlin and Ethan headed in the direction of the office.

"Do you think they'll be all right?" she asked. Old habits were hard to break.

"They'll be fine."

Caitlin sat on the top porch step, keeping Justin in sight, but not fretting about him. Not like she had, anyway.

Ethan lowered himself down beside her, his movements still stiff.

"How are you doing?"

"Better. The doctor suggested physical therapy. Know a good therapist?"

"I might."

They both laughed and, just like that, the tension between them evaporated.

"You first," she said.

He took a moment before continuing. "Being laid up the last couple of weeks has given me a lot of time to think. About my job. About rodeoing. About us." He cleared his throat. "I've made a decision."

His tone was so serious. Had she misinterpreted his intentions? Good heavens. He was breaking up with her. Now, after she'd finally come to her senses.

"I love you," she blurted.

"Good." He sagged with obvious relief. "That makes what I'm going to tell you a whole lot easier." He fitted his palm to her cheek and rubbed his thumb along her jawline. "After my discharge, I wanted to…needed to ride broncs. To prove to myself and everyone else I was the same man I'd been before I lost my leg."

"I understand. And you don't have to give up rodeoing for me."

"I want to." His dark eyes searched hers. "It isn't important to me anymore. Having you, loving you, is. Nothing I do matters without you in my life. You make me the man I want to be. If Justin hadn't tricked you into coming here today, I would have gone after you myself and begged you to give us a second chance." He chuckled. "Guess that would be a third chance."

"Justin tricked me?" She tried to be mad at her brother but couldn't. "Remind me to thank him."

Ethan cupped her other cheek and held her face between his hands. "If you'll have me, I'll also give up breaking horses."

"That's your job."

"I'll find another one."

"Not on your life, cowboy, you hear me? You're a Powell."

"Caitlin, baby doll—"

"No. Quitting bronc riding is enough." She remembered Justin's words. "I can handle breaking horses, though. I'll need help. Lots of support and understanding."

"You'll have it."

He kissed her then, and it was the sweetest kiss he'd ever given her.

"Life is full of risks," she said dreamily. "And they're not all bad."

She'd taken a huge one minutes ago when she'd asked to talk to him, and it was already paying off.

"Marry me, Caitlin. I love you, too."

Her eyes went wide. "What did you say?"

"I'd get down on one knee, except between my bum leg and broken ribs, I'm not sure I could get back up."

She drew in a ragged breath, her earlier indecision fleeing. "There's something you need to know first."

"If you're worried about honing in on Gavin and Sage's wedding next month, I can wait. Not long, mind you."

"It's not that."

"We'll buy a ring. Sorry I proposed without one."

"No, no, no. I don't care about a ring. Well, I do, but not this second."

"Then what?"

"Marriage is life changing." She wavered, scared and yet bursting with excitement. "Having a baby is, too."

He stared at her blankly.

She huffed impatiently. Did she have to spell it out? "I'm pregnant."

His dumbfounded expression transformed into one of unabashed delight.

Ethan struggled to his feet. He barely made it and doubled over, a low sound exploding from him.

"Ethan, are you all right?" She was instantly up and grabbed his arm.

"My ribs." He was laughing, and the sound grew louder as he straightened.

She laughed with him.

Gavin threw open the office door. Caitlin hadn't realized he was in there.

"What's going on?" His glance traveled from Ethan to Caitlin. "I take it you two are back together."

"More than back together." Ethan stopped laughing and pulled Caitlin to him. "You did accept, didn't you?"

"Yes, I'll marry you." She put her arms around him gently drunk on happiness.

Gavin barreled down the steps and embraced them both, ignoring Ethan's protest to take it easy. "It's about damn time."

Justin and Tamiko came over, her brother still mounted. "What's going on?" he asked.

Ethan let go of Caitlin and shouted through cupped hands loudly enough for the entire ranch to hear, "We're getting hitched and we're having a baby."

After that, everything was a blur. Caitlin was aware of hugs and kisses and lots of congratulations. Wayne Powell suddenly appeared. He must have come out of the house to investigate all the commotion. Sage and the girls were with him.

"Ethan's mother would be so happy." Wayne kissed Caitlin on the cheek. "Another grandchild."

Someone had helped Justin down from the horse, for he was suddenly in his wheelchair. He held her fiercely when she leaned down to hug him.

"Thanks," she whispered. "For the advice and for tricking me into coming here. You're the best."

"Anytime, sis."

"Guess I'd better let Mom and Dad know."

Ethan put an arm around her. "We'll drive out there later. Tell them together."

She beamed at him. "Really?" That was exactly the right thing to do.

"You could have a double wedding," Tamiko suggested gleefully, then reddened when everyone stared at her.

Ethan found his voice first. "What do you think? I know it's kind of short notice."

Caitlin could tell by his eager grin that he liked the idea. He'd want to get married as soon as possible, what with the baby coming. "Gavin and Sage may not want—"

"Gavin and Sage *absolutely* want," Sage answered for them both. "All the arrangements are under way. It makes perfect sense."

"Okay." Caitlin shrugged, suddenly warming to the idea, as well. "Let's have a double wedding."

They took their celebrating inside to continue over supper.

Caitlin sat at the kitchen table next to Ethan, across from her brother, and with the family that had come to mean as much to her as her own.

When the meal was nearing an end, Wayne tapped his water glass with his fork. Everyone fell silent. "Here's to my second future daughter-in-law. Welcome to the Powell family." Wayne smiled at Caitlin affectionately. "I've been waiting nine years to say that."

She'd been waiting nine years to hear it.

The passage of time, the trials and tribulations she and Ethan had confronted and conquered, made the moment all the more meaningful.

Christmas wishes could and did come true.

Beneath the table, Ethan took her hand and linked their fingers. *"Stay with me tonight,"* he mouthed.

As if she would ever leave him or this place again.

* * * * *

HEART & HOME

Heartwarming romances where love can
happen right when you least expect it.

Harlequin®

American ★ Romance®

COMING NEXT MONTH
AVAILABLE JANUARY 10, 2012

#1385 HIS VALENTINE TRIPLETS
Callahan Cowboys
Tina Leonard

#1386 THE COWBOY'S SECRET SON
The Teagues of Texas
Trish Milburn

#1387 THE SEAL'S PROMISE
Undercover Heroes
Rebecca Winters

#1388 CLAIMED BY A COWBOY
Hill Country Heroes
Tanya Michaels

REQUEST YOUR FREE BOOKS!

2 FREE NOVELS PLUS 2 FREE GIFTS!

Harlequin

American ★ Romance

LOVE, HOME & HAPPINESS

YES! Please send me 2 FREE Harlequin® American Romance® novels and my 2 FREE gifts (gifts are worth about $10). After receiving them, if I don't wish to receive any more books, I can return the shipping statement marked "cancel." If I don't cancel, I will receive 4 brand-new novels every month and be billed just $4.49 per book in the U.S. or $5.24 per book in Canada. That's a saving of at least 14% off the cover price! It's quite a bargain! Shipping and handling is just 50¢ per book in the U.S. and 75¢ per book in Canada.* I understand that accepting the 2 free books and gifts places me under no obligation to buy anything. I can always return a shipment and cancel at any time. Even if I never buy another book, the two free books and gifts are mine to keep forever.

154/354 HDN FEP2

Name	(PLEASE PRINT)	

Address		Apt. #

City	State/Prov.	Zip/Postal Code

Signature (if under 18, a parent or guardian must sign)

Mail to the **Reader Service:**
IN U.S.A.: P.O. Box 1867, Buffalo, NY 14240-1867
IN CANADA: P.O. Box 609, Fort Erie, Ontario L2A 5X3

Not valid for current subscribers to Harlequin American Romance books.

**Want to try two free books from another line?
Call 1-800-873-8635 or visit www.ReaderService.com.**

* Terms and prices subject to change without notice. Prices do not include applicable taxes. Sales tax applicable in N.Y. Canadian residents will be charged applicable taxes. Offer not valid in Quebec. This offer is limited to one order per household. All orders subject to credit approval. Credit or debit balances in a customer's account(s) may be offset by any other outstanding balance owed by or to the customer. Please allow 4 to 6 weeks for delivery. Offer available while quantities last.

Your Privacy—The Reader Service is committed to protecting your privacy. Our Privacy Policy is available online at www.ReaderService.com or upon request from the Reader Service.

We make a portion of our mailing list available to reputable third parties that offer products we believe may interest you. If you prefer that we not exchange your name with third parties, or if you wish to clarify or modify your communication preferences, please visit us at www.ReaderService.com/consumerchoice or write to us at Reader Service Preference Service, P.O. Box 9062, Buffalo, NY 14269. Include your complete name and address.

SPECIAL EDITION

Life, Love and Family

Karen Templeton

introduces

The FORTUNES *of* TEXAS: Whirlwind Romance

When a tornado destroys Red Rock, Texas, Christina Hastings finds herself trapped in the rubble with telecommunications heir Scott Fortune. He's handsome, smart and everything Christina has learned to guard herself against. As they await rescue, an unlikely attraction forms between the two and Scott soon finds himself wanting to know about this mysterious beauty. But can he catch Christina before she runs away from her true feelings?

FORTUNE'S CINDERELLA

Available December 27th wherever books are sold!

Brittany Grayson survived a horrible ordeal at the hands of a serial killer known as The Professional... who's after her now?

Harlequin® Romantic Suspense presents a new installment in Carla Cassidy's reader-favorite miniseries,
LAWMEN OF BLACK ROCK.

Enjoy a sneak peek of
TOOL BELT DEFENDER.

Available January 2012
from Harlequin® Romantic Suspense.

"**B**rittany?" His voice was deep and pleasant and made her realize she'd been staring at him openmouthed through the screen door.

"Yes, I'm Brittany and you must be..." Her mind suddenly went blank.

"Alex. Alex Crawford, Chad's friend. You called him about a deck?"

As she unlocked the screen, she realized she wasn't quite ready yet to allow a stranger inside, especially a male stranger.

"Yes, I did. It's nice to meet you, Alex. Let's walk around back and I'll show you what I have in mind," she said. She frowned as she realized there was no car in her driveway. "Did you walk here?" she asked.

His eyes were a warm blue that stood out against his tanned face and was complemented by his slightly shaggy dark hair. "I live three doors up." He pointed up the street to the Walker home that had been on the market for a while.

"How long have you lived there?"

"I moved in about six weeks ago," he replied as they

walked around the side of the house.

That explained why she didn't know the Walkers had moved out and Mr. Hard Body had moved in. Six weeks ago she'd still been living at her brother Benjamin's house trying to heal from the trauma she'd lived through.

As they reached the backyard she motioned toward the broken brick patio just outside the back door. "What I'd like is a wooden deck big enough to hold a barbecue pit and an umbrella table and, of course, lots of people."

He nodded and pulled a tape measure from his tool belt. "An outdoor entertainment area," he said.

"Exactly," she replied and watched as he began to walk the site. The last thing Brittany had wanted to think about over the past eight months of her life was men. But looking at Alex Crawford definitely gave her a slight flutter of pure feminine pleasure.

Will Brittany be able to heal in the arms of Alex,
her hotter-than-sin handyman...or will a second
psychopath silence her forever? Find out in
TOOL BELT DEFENDER
Available January 2012
from Harlequin® Romantic Suspense
wherever books are sold.

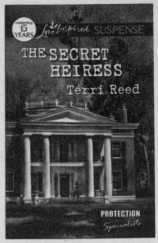